WESTERN

W9-BXL-685

RENEGADE RIFLES

This Large Print Book carries the
Seal of Approval of N.A.V.H.

THE TRAILSMAN: RENEGADE RIFLES

Jon Sharpe

Thorndike Press • Thorndike, Maine

The first chapter of this book previously appeared in *Arizona Slaughter*, the one hundred eighteenth volume in this series.

Published in 2000 by arrangement with Signet, a division of Penguin Putnam, Inc.

Thorndike Press Large Print Western Series.

The tree indicium is a trademark of Thorndike Press.

The text of this Large Print edition is unabridged. Other aspects of the book may vary from the original edition.

Set in 16 pt. Plantin by Rick Gundberg.

Printed in the United States on permanent paper.

Library of Congress Cataloging-in-Publication Data

Sharpe, Jon.
   Renegade rifles / by Jon Sharpe.
    p. cm.
   Originally published as The trailsman no. 119.
   ISBN 0-7862-2588-2 (lg. print : hc : alk. paper)
   1. Oklahoma — Fiction. 2. Large type books. I. Title.
II. Trailsman; no. 119.
PS3561.N645 R46 2000
  813'.54—dc21
                                        00-023472

The Trailsman

Beginnings . . . they bend the tree and they mark the man. Skye Fargo was born when he was eighteen. Terror was his midwife, vengeance his first cry. Killing spawned Skye Fargo, ruthless, cold-blooded murder. Out of the acrid smoke of gunpowder still hanging in the air, he rose, cried out a promise never forgotten.

The Trailsman they began to call him all across the West: searcher, scout, hunter, the man who could see where others only looked, his skills for hire but not his soul, the man who lived each day to the fullest, yet trailed each tomorrow. Skye Fargo, the Trailsman, the seeker who could take the wildness of a land and the wanting of a woman and make them his own.

1860, just south of the Salt Fork Red, in the land the government called the Indian Territory but the settlers called hell's empire . . .

1

His first glimpse of the young woman was a figure sliding down an embankment. She landed at the bottom and he waited to see if a horse followed her. But nothing else slid down the steep side of the embankment and he watched the young woman pick herself up and begin to run toward a thick stand of blackjack oak.

She ran with terror in her every movement, legs driving, arms held stiffly, casting quick glances behind her. Tall, with dusty-blond hair flowing out behind her, a torn brown dress allowed glimpses of strong, shapely legs. The big man's lake-blue eyes narrowed as he watched her disappear into the oak. She was plainly running from something and he stayed unmoving in the saddle. The stand of oak was short. She'd be at the other end in minutes. He moved forward a few paces but stayed inside the cluster of box elder.

He had spent the day riding leisurely northward, up from Quanah, letting the magnificent Ovaro set its own pace, the animal's jet-black fore and hindquarters and pure white midsection glistening in the hot sun. Now he moved another few paces inside the trees and the young woman flashed into sight. She paused to catch her breath and glanced fearfully right and left before turning to run toward a larger and thicker stand of oak. Then suddenly he saw why she fled as the three small but sturdy Indian ponies appeared atop a low rise of land, each carrying a bare-chested rider. The three bucks halted, their eyes sweeping the terrain. It took only a moment for them to find their quarry as the sunlight caught the dusty-blond hair in a yellow flash against the dark green foliage.

Skye Fargo leaned forward in the saddle as the young woman saw the three figures start to move after her along the top of the rise. She tried to run faster and only succeeded in stumbling and falling forward. She picked herself up at once and started for the stand of oaks. But the fall had cost her almost a half minute and the three Indians were halfway down the slope now. Fargo's eyes went to the oaks and back to the girl. She'd never reach the trees in time, he was certain. He spurred the Ovaro forward toward the fleeing girl. But he stayed in the trees that stretched out before him until they joined the main stand of oaks. The treeline curved and took him a dozen yards from the fleeing figure. He had to stay inside the cover and a quick glance backward showed him the three bucks were on the level ground now, their ponies going full out.

Fargo's hand reached down to the big Colt at his side but he quickly let the gun drop back into its holster. The three bucks might not be alone. Shots would surely bring any others nearby. He kept the pinto running through the trees as his eyes went to the three Indians that were almost abreast of him, now. Each carried a rifle, he saw, one a new Henry and the other two Smith & Wesson Volcanics. His eyes switched to the young woman. She was nearing the oaks but she was running out of time, the three bucks closing in fast now. Fargo brought his concentration back to skirting tree trunks as he put the Ovaro into a gallop and he reached the place where his tree cover joined the heavy stand of oak. He raced into the oak, slowed and saw that the three horsemen had reached the fleeing young woman, not more than a dozen yards from where he was inside the trees.

One bent low from the back of his pony, reached out and grabbed a handful of the dusty-blond hair. The young woman screamed in pain as he yanked her back and flung her to the ground. The other two were already off their ponies and seized her at once. One, a

11

narrow-framed buck with his thick, black hair in two braids, pulled the girl to her feet, a grin of anticipation on his face. The third buck had dismounted and stepped up to pull the young woman's head up and backward. She was good-looking, Fargo noted, high-cheek-boned with a small nose and a face that held strength even in pain and fright.

Fargo reined to a halt inside the oak stand, the trio holding the girl directly in front of him. His eyes swept the scene, taking in every detail of the three Indians with the precise absorption that was an automatic thing, as much a part of him as breathing. He felt the frown dig into his brow for a moment as he dropped to the ground on the balls of his feet with the silence of a mountain cat. He knelt, reached down and drew the knife from the narrow leather holster he wore around his calf. He turned the blade in his hand, a perfectly balanced throwing knife, thin and double-edged with each edge razor sharp, the kind often called an Arkansas toothpick.

He moved forward, to the very edge of the trees as two of the bucks threw the young woman on the ground. She kicked out with both legs and again he saw long, lovely limbs. The third brave fell atop her, pressing her legs apart as the other two held her arms stretched upward. The buck wore loose cotton leggings of the kind favored by the Apache and he had the front open in seconds as he reached up to tear the young woman's underclothes away. He was laughing and his companions joined in with deep, grunting sounds, a kind of obscene cheerleading. Fargo chose the one holding the girl's right arm, took another half-second to aim and sent the blade hurtling through the air with all the power of arm and shoulder muscles.

He watched the blade slam into the center of the man's chest and bury itself up to the hilt. The Indian dropped his hands from the young woman's arm as he staggered backward. Surprise flooded his face first, utter and total surprise as he looked down at the knife hilt in his chest. The pain came next as his mouth fell open and his eyes grew wide. He staggered back another two steps, tried to pull the blade from the chest but the hand that closed around the hilt of the knife had already lost its strength. Slowly, with a half-spiral, he sank to the ground and lay still.

Fargo's eyes went to the other two bucks. Both had let go of the young woman and were frozen in a half-crouch, rifles raised, peering into the trees. A sudden and complete silence had descended on the scene, even the young woman frozen in place as she lay propped up on her elbows. The two braves were listening,

Fargo realized, as he remained equally silent and motionless. He saw one of them flick his hand, a quick leftward motion and the other one immediately darted away in a crouch. He ran for the trees while the first one ran to the other side.

Both moved into the oaks, one to his left, one to his right and Fargo glanced at the young woman again. She was sitting up but she hadn't tried to run again, her eyes wide and fearful as she watched the two Indians move into the trees. Surprise and fear still held her frozen and he returned his attention to the trees. The two bucks stayed silent and unmoving for a full two minutes, straining their ears. But Fargo stayed equally silent in the high brush, hardly breathing. The two braves started to move, a dozen darting steps and then a pause to listen again, waiting to pick up a telltale sound, the movement of brush, the soft sound of dirt being scraped by a footstep. Fargo's smile was thin. This time their quarry could think as well as react by instinct.

He chose the brave to his right, gathered his muscles and he was ready when the Indian moved again. Fargo moved at the same time. When the Indian halted, he halted, too. The buck moved again and Fargo moved with him, using the Indian's movements as cover for his own. Once again the buck halted to listen and once again he heard nothing. But he was close now. Fargo could see him through the foliage. The other one was still a fair distance away and Fargo's concentration was focused on the nearest buck. The Indian moved again, another dozen quick steps, and then dropped to one knee to listen for the sound of his quarry. But again Fargo had moved with him. He was almost directly behind the Indian, now. He knew he'd have but one chance to strike and make the strike swift and noiseless.

He rose up on the balls of his feet, not unlike a runner at the starting line. The buck was in front of him, listening as he peered through the trees. He had a rifle in one hand, held near to his side. Fargo rose up and dove forward in one motion as fluid as water leaving the neck of a jar. The buck caught the movement of air behind him, started to spin but Fargo was on him, one hand closing around the rifle at the breech. He brought the gun upward, closed his other hand around the end of the barrel and jammed the gun horizontally against the buck's throat as he pulled backward. The Indian fell against him as Fargo pulled against the rifle again and felt the man's throat collapse inward.

The buck slid down to the ground as Fargo

15

pulled the rifle from his throat. It had taken not more than a half-dozen seconds and it had been almost noiseless, just the rustle of brush and the tiny gasped choke. But almost wasn't good enough. The other buck had heard and Fargo heard him charging. The Trailsman spun as the Indian raised his rifle and fired, still charging, the shot too hasty, the bullet too high. Fargo dipped as he brought up a left hook in a blazing arc. The Indian was still charging as the blow smashed into his jaw and Fargo heard the sound of bone cracking.

. The buck stopped as though he had run into a stone wall. The rifle dropped from his hand and Fargo caught it before it hit the ground. He smashed the heavy stock across the man's head as the Indian was already collapsing. The blow ensured he'd not get up again and Fargo spun away with a silent curse of his lips. The Indian had gotten off one shot and that could be more than enough. He ran from the trees to see the young woman on her feet and starting to flee. She halted when he called out, turned and saw him and a wave of relief flooded her face.

She was more attractive than he'd been able to see — full lips, a tall frame with full breasts and hazel eyes that held a direct, strong stare. She ran toward him and he caught her by the arm. "Into the trees. That shot could bring more," he said.

"No, those three were the only ones chasing me," she said. "The others are half a mile away, attacking the wagons. I was running to find help." Fargo gave a low whistle and the Ovaro trotted from the trees. "You've got to go back with me and help those poor people in the wagons," the young woman said. He nodded but paused to kneel down beside the first buck and pull his knife free, his eyes sweeping the prostrate form of the Indian as he cleaned the blade on the grass. Once again, he felt the furrow cross his brow but he rose, swung onto the Ovaro and pulled the young woman up behind him in the saddle.

Her arms went around his waist and he felt the warmth of her against his back. She smelled of perspiration and powder, a musky, dark odor that was strangely attractive. "Which way?" he asked.

"North, over the ridge and across the next hill," she said.

"How'd you get away?" he asked as he put the pinto into a gallop and felt her breasts bouncing against him.

"We had stopped. I'd gone off to pick berries when they attacked. I hid, at first, and then tried to run. But those three saw me and came after me. Maybe if I'd had a horse I could've gotten away from them."

"Just the opposite," Fargo said. "You managed to avoid being caught for as long as you did because you were on foot. They'd have caught you real quick if you'd been on horseback."

"You might be right. I was able to go into every little crevice and gully. I thought I'd gotten away from them at one point but then they spotted me again," she said. Fargo fell silent, concentrated on riding hard and felt her arms pull tighter around his waist. He kept the Ovaro at a gallop as he climbed the first low hill, then the second and slowed as he neared the crest. A quick glance skyward showed him that there weren't more than two hours of daylight left. He heard the wild whoops, unmistakable and always chilling, as he crested the hill. An expanse of post oak swept down the hill to let him keep racing forward until he drew closer to the bottom.

He saw the wagons, then, three of them, halted against a line of cottonwoods. He halted beneath one of the oaks and slid from the saddle, the girl coming with him. He dropped to one knee as his gaze swept the scene. Some two dozen bucks, he counted, exuberantly racing back and forth alongside the wagons. The attack was over, a half-dozen bodies hanging over the sides of the three

Conestogas. "What are you stopping here for?" he heard the young woman ask. "We've got to go down and help them."

"It's too late," Fargo said grimly.

"You don't know that."

"I know it," he said.

"We can't just sit here and watch. Shoot some of them. Chase them away. Do something, damn you," she said and he saw her face was white with strain, her hands clenched into fists.

"That'd be committing suicide, nothing more," he said.

"Why'd you come then if you weren't going to help?" she flung at him, fury in her hazel eyes.

"I hoped I could help. I might have, if the fight was still going on. But not now. It's too late," he said.

"It's not too late for me," she snapped and spun on her heel, yanked the rifle from the saddle holster of the Ovaro and started to bring the gun around. She was upset beyond reason, caught up in the kind of fury and anguish that snaps the mind. He leaped, twisted the rifle from her hands and his blow just grazed the tip of her pretty chin. But it was enough and he saw her eyes flutter shut as she started to go down. He caught her with one arm and lowered her gently to the ground.

Jamming the rifle back into its holster, he returned to one knee and watched the scene at the now silent wagons. The furrow that had touched his brow earlier returned, but now as a full-fledged frown. The braves had dismounted and three tore the canvas top from the lead Conestoga, then ripped the arched bows away to allow more room inside the wagon. Fargo's frown grew even deeper as he saw other braves carry lamps, small dressers, pots and pans, a bedstand table plus the headboard and footboard of a bed, another larger dresser and finally a sewing machine from the other two wagons and load everything into the first.

While he watched in consternation, one brave took the reins of the Conestoga and began to drive the wagon upward along a shallow while the others rode their ponies alongside. He was watching them move away when the small groan broke into his thoughts and he turned to see the young woman stir, pull her eyes open and sit up. She stared at him for a moment and her open-handed slap grazed the side of his cheek as he just managed to pull back in time. "Bastard. Coward," she hissed.

He caught her wrist and yanked her around hard so she could see the last of the Indians disappear into the trees. "It's done, finished,

dammit," he hissed. "No more out of you."
She glared at him as he let her wrist go.
"Damnedest thing I've ever seen. I'm thinking about following them," he said. "There's
only a half hour of daylight left."

"There could be people still alive in the
wagons," she said. "Alive enough to get to
town and a doctor. That's more important
than chasing after those savages."

"Red Sand's the nearest town. That's a good
ten miles north into Oklahoma Territory," he
said.

"That's where we were going," she said. He
drew a deep sigh and met her pain-filled anger
with a grimace. There was a glimmer of truth
in her words. There was always that chance
that life still flickered. He rose, pulled her to
her feet and began to walk down the hill toward
the wagons, the Ovaro following behind. She
caught up to him to walk beside him. The
furrow was still digging into his brow when he
reached the remaining two wagons and he cast
a quick glance at the young woman. She had
steeled herself for what they saw — jaw tight,
shoulders thrown back and her full breasts
straining the top of the brown dress. She had
her own determined strength, he saw, no
flinching in her as she halted beside the ar-
row-riddled bodies.

He had seen worse. There'd been no time

for mutilation and there were only three scalpings. He walked slowly among the bodies littering the ground and pulled the canvas back on each wagon to look at those still inside. The young woman stayed with him and he heard her quick, sharp gasps of breath. Finally he halted and turned to her. None were clinging to life. "There were three children, two boys and a girl," she said. "They're not here. You think they got away?"

He shook his head. "How old were they?"

"Nine to eleven," she said.

"They were taken off before we got here," he said.

"Oh, God," she breathed. "I've heard that happens."

"It does. It's the only thing about this that fits," he said and she frowned back.

"Meaning what?" she asked.

"I don't know what," Fargo said as dusk began to roll across the dip of land. "I'll take you to Red Sand."

"You sure it won't inconvenience you," she said, an edge of disdain suddenly in her voice.

"Watch your damn tongue, honey," Fargo said. "Or I might just leave you to walk."

"That wouldn't surprise me," she sniffed and he fastened her with a glare.

"You still stewing because I wouldn't rush in shooting like a damn fool?" he questioned.

"Yes. Maybe it'd have saved one life," she snapped.

"It'd have ended mine," he said. "And yours." She glared back, refusing to concede. "You can think whatever the hell you like about me, honey. I don't give a damn." He spun from her and pulled himself onto the Ovaro.

"No, I don't suppose you do," she said.

"I saved your ass and your scalp," he said. "You can remember that while you're walking." He turned the Ovaro, flicked the reins and the horse started off.

"Wait," he heard the young woman call out and he reined to a halt. She hurried up to him. "You did," she said, the anger out of her face. "Maybe I've been too harsh."

"Maybe?" he echoed.

Her lips tightened. "All right, no maybe. I was too harsh."

"Try adding stupid," he said, waited, his face set.

Her eyes glared. "You enjoy humiliating someone?" she said.

"I enjoy truth," he said coldly.

She drew a deep breath, her breasts rising beautifully. "All right. I was harsh and stupid. You feel better now?" she asked.

"No, but you should," he answered and she stared back for a long moment.

"Nobody's ever talked that way to me before," she said slowly.

"Too bad," he grunted and reached his hand out. She closed her fingers around his and he pulled her into the saddle, in front of him, this time. The darkness descended as he rode from the dip in the land and the furrow on his brow returned. It had nothing to do with the young woman leaning back against him. But maybe she knew more than she realized. He'd try to find out on the way to Red Sand.

2

A half-moon rose as Fargo moved the Ovaro across the land beyond the hills, into terrain where rock formations rose up along one side. "You've got a name?" he grunted.

"Jennifer Latham," she said. "And you?"

"Fargo — Skye Fargo. Some call me the Trailsman," he answered.

"Is that what you were doing out here? Breaking trail?" Jennifer Latham asked.

"No, I just finished a job, all the way down to Abilene. I was heading back north," he told her. "You know anybody well on that wagon train? You have kin on it?"

"No. I was traveling alone," she said.

"To Red Sand?"

"Yes, to my Uncle Aran. His place is somewhere outside town I'm told," Jennifer said.

"Then he's expecting you."

"Well, yes and no."

"That's an answer that doesn't answer much."

"I don't want to go into more now."

"You know where the other folks on the

train were heading?" Fargo questioned.

"The train was to stop over at Red Sand and then go north and eventually hook up with the Gila River trail into Utah territory," she said.

"You saw nothing special about anybody on the wagons?"

"No, they were pretty much ordinary folks. Why all the questions?" Jennifer frowned.

He felt his lips pull back. "I guess I'm just looking for something to help me understand what I don't understand," he said.

"Talk about answers that don't answer much," she sniffed. He uttered a wry sound and wished he had something better to give. The land rose and the rock formations to one side reached closer. Suddenly he yanked the horse to a halt, sound reaching him before sight. Moments later he saw four riders coming over the top of a low hill. They spread out, moonlight glistening on their near-naked bodies.

Fargo swerved the Ovaro sharply right. He was inside a narrow crevice in seconds, rocky sides with an outgrowth of hard, rugged brush. He let the horse go deeper before he halted and slid from the saddle to stand still. He listened, letting his wild-creature hearing pick up the sounds of hoofbeats, some receding, others growing clearer. "They're making a wide sweep," he said. "Looking for the three that didn't show. They won't hear any cries for help and they won't find them in the dark."

"What then?" Jennifer asked.

"They'll break off the search. We stay here till then," he said. He slid down to the ground, his back against the flat side of rock. Jennifer lowered herself to sit a few feet from him. The torn dress let him see the loveliness of a long thigh as she leaned her head back against the rock. The moonlight caught her strong cheekbones and even features in its silvery light. She was an uncommonly attractive young woman, he decided, even with the touch of arrogance that stayed in her face.

"I left all my things back in the wagons," she said. "I didn't think about anything but getting away from that terrible scene."

"I imagine they'll send a burying party from Red Sand. It's not too far. They can pick up your things," Fargo said.

"I never expected to find myself in anything like this," Jennifer said and Fargo felt the irritation rise up inside him.

"Why not? You think Indian Territory was a place for lawn parties?" he snapped.

"No, but somehow you always think of things like this happening to somebody else," she said.

"Not if you've any damn sense," he growled and her lips tightened.

"Why are you so harsh?" she accused.

"Because I've seen too much of that kind of thinking. It brings trouble, for those who do it and for those around them. This is no land for safe, comforting thinking. You think the worst and stay alert. That can spell the difference between living and dying," Fargo said and she fell silent. "Where do you hail from?" he questioned.

"Kentucky, just south of Lake Cumberland," she said.

"You come this way to visit or set down roots?" he asked.

"Visit, first. Maybe the roots will come later," she said. He pushed to his feet to stand motionless, holding his breath as he listened. Finally he let his breath out in a slow slide of air.

"I think they've gone. Let's ride," he said. Jennifer pulled herself onto the Ovaro and he climbed on behind her. He felt the very soft sides of her breasts as he reached around her to hold the reins. He continued to listen as he nosed the pinto out of the crevice but the night stayed silent. He put the horse into a trot when he reached flat land. The moon was nearing the midnight sky when the low, flat-roofed structures of Red Sand came into view. The town had thrived as a way station for settlers from the south and the southeast — eager, striving wagonloads of families on their way to explored trails that led westward. Some would take the Santa Fe trail but most would go north to the Mormon and Oregon trails. The town had spawned some permanent settlements around it but it existed mainly on the traffic of those who paused there on their way someplace else.

"You know where your uncle's place is?" Fargo asked as he rode into the dark streets.

"Haven't any idea," Jennifer said. He pulled to a halt in front of the only lighted building in town where the tinkling sound of a piano and the smoke-filled air drifted into the street.

"What's his name?" Fargo asked as he slid to the ground.

"Aran Tooney," Jennifer said. He left her to return in a few moments and climb into the saddle again.

"West, over the first low hill," he said and put the Ovaro into a trot. He moved along a road out of town, stayed on it as it curved west and finally spied a low hill. The ranch came into sight on the other side in a hollow of land — three outbuildings beyond the main ranchhouse and two large corrals. A light still burned in the ranchhouse, he saw. When he pulled up to the front door, he swung to the ground with Jennifer. He waited beside her as she knocked. When the door pulled open, he saw a fair-sized man made paunchy by some thirty unneeded pounds, a face made fleshy by heavy jowls, and topped by unruly salt-and-pepper hair. Wearing red suspenders over a white shirt and baggy trousers, the man stared at the young woman.

Fargo watched his mouth drop open as disbelief flooded his fleshy face. "It's me, Uncle Aran," Jennifer said and Fargo saw shock push aside disbelief in the man's slightly watery blue eyes.

"Jennifer. My God, Jennifer," Aran Tooney breathed. "What are you doing here now?"

"Changed my plans," Jennifer said and beckoned to Fargo to follow as she stepped into the house.

"You were due on the stage from Fayetville next week," Aran Tooney said. "I was going to send men to meet you."

"I was early. The stage wouldn't have left for another two weeks. I paid my way onto a wagon train I heard was coming here. I thought I'd surprise you," Jennifer said.

"A wagon train," her uncle echoed as he stared at her.

Jennifer's face grew grave. "It turned out horribly. We were attacked. I'd be dead if it wasn't for this man," she said and Aran Tooney's eyes went to the big man standing beside his niece.

"Name's Fargo — Skye Fargo," the Trailsman said and Aran Tooney nodded as he lowered himself onto the edge of a worn couch. He listened as Jennifer told what had happened and his face was chalk white when she finished.

"My God, Jennifer, my God," he murmured, and then, an edge of anger came into his voice. "That's why I arranged for you to come by stage. The stages aren't attacked like the wagon trains."

"I'm sorry. I thought I was doing something good," Jennifer said. Aran Tooney stared into space for another long moment, his brow wrinkled.

"You've a sheriff here?" Fargo asked.

"We've been lucky. Haven't had much need for a sheriff. Mayor Gibson doubles if he has to," the man said.

"It's late now. What I have to say can wait till morning," Fargo said. "Where'll I find him?"

"Mayor's office, right in the center of town," the man said as he rose to his feet. "You're welcome to stay. There's plenty of room."

"Some other time, maybe," Fargo said.

"I'm sure grateful to you for seeing that Jennifer's alive," the man said as Fargo turned to go.

"I'll see Fargo out," Jennifer said, brushing past her uncle. She walked to the Ovaro, her hazel eyes searching the big man's face. "What is it you want to talk to the mayor about?" she asked.

"Got a few questions," he said.

"About whatever it is that you don't understand?" she pressed.

"That's part of it," he said.

"Can I come listen?" she asked. "I want to see about getting my bags, too."

"Why not? You were part of it," he said. "I'll see you come morning, around nine o'clock give or take."

Her hand reached out, rested on his arm as he started to climb onto the horse. "I won't sleep very well tonight. I'll be thinking about everything that happened and what you did for me. I won't be forgetting either," she said. She reached up, a quick, unexpected motion and he felt her lips on his, a fleeting softness and then she pulled back. "For the things I said which I shouldn't have said," she murmured.

"Fair enough." He smiled and watched ᴜrn and go into the house, her long back ʀy straight. There was no giving in to

32

what she had just been through, her body reflecting her spirit. She had her own strength, he decided as he rode across the hills, up a slightly higher rise of land and halted beneath a widespread cottonwood that let him gaze across the moon-swept terrain. This was a land rugged in more ways than its sand dunes, pitted outwashes, sandstone buttresses, burning sun and strands of dense forests. It was a battleground for numerous tribes: The Kiowa ruling the north, Comanche coming up from the south and the Cheyenne making forays in from the west. They were but a few of the many in this land that spread over Oklahoma, Texas, parts of Kansas and New Mexico.

The government called it the Indian Territory because they'd once ceded it to several of the tribes and then promptly encouraged settlers to move in. That's when the name took on the face of savagery, deceit and fury. But Fargo grimaced as he set out his bedroll and undressed. None of the region's bloodstained history gave any explanation for what he had witnessed and he went to sleep with the hope that the new day might offer some answers. He slept soundly and woke when the morning sun pressed its way through the large, triangular leaves of the big cottonwood. He used his canteen to wash and found a persimmon tree that provided a tasty breakfast as he rode to Red Sand.

The town was active, the merchants all open and busy when he entered the wide main street. Texas cotton-bed wagons and Conestogas shouldered each other, with a few platform spring drays outfitted with bows and canvas tops. He saw a good number of ladies in town clothes who were plainly residents of the region and a few youngsters, some from the parked Conestogas. He found the mayor's office in the center of town where Jennifer's uncle had said it would be, a modest storefront with a buckboard outside. He felt a moment of surprise when he entered the office and saw Jennifer already there. She rose to greet him at once.

She wore the same torn brown dress, he noted, but the dusty-blond hair had been washed and brushed to a quiet glow and her hazel eyes were less troubled as they smiled at him. Aran Tooney sat in a chair beside her, red suspenders over a freshly pressed white shirt. Fargo's eyes went to the man that rose from behind a wooden desk. He saw a diminutive figure, not more than five-foot-five inches tall, he estimated, clad in a gray jacket and cravat. But a ruddy, animated face with close-cropped brown hair and sharp blue eyes gave the man an air of decisiveness that made him seem less small than he was.

"Welcome, Fargo. Jennifer has told me what you did for her yesterday," the man said. "I'm Mayor Gibson — Hal Gibson."

"Thought I'd drive Jennifer into town," Aran Tooney said.

Jennifer stepped forward to rest one hand on Fargo's arm. "The mayor has already sent out a burying party. They'll bring my bags back so I'll have something to wear beside this torn dress," she said.

"Damn terrible business, these attacks," the mayor said. "Jennifer said you were bothered by something about this one."

"It wasn't like any Indian attack I've ever seen," Fargo said and saw Mayor Gibson's brows lift. "Indians will strip their victims of boots, belts, sometimes clothes — mostly women's, and knives and guns. They'll take hair combs, trinkets, and mirrors, but they leave the rest. These took household objects — dressers, end tables, lamps, even a sewing machine. Damnedest thing I ever saw."

"That's been the case with almost every wagon train attacked lately. We can see where things have been taken from the wagons when we come onto them," the mayor said.

"It doesn't add up," Fargo said.

"Seems simple to me. The damn savages have just taken a liking to the white man's trappings," Aran Tooney said.

"Tables to use in tepees? Sewing machines to carry on the long winter treks?" Fargo said with some annoyance and Aran Tooney shrugged. "Besides, there was something else," Fargo added.

"Something else?" the mayor echoed.

"One brave had definite Kiowa markings on his armband. I saw another with Cheyenne designs on his moccasins and I could swear I saw Wichita marks on another's pouch," Fargo said. "I know these tribes are part of those in Indian territory but they hate each other almost as much as they do the white man. Yet here were three working together."

"That couldn't be. You must've seen wrong," Hal Gibson said.

Aran Tooney's voice cut in. "Or one of them found an armband and decided to wear it," the man offered.

"No Indian would wear another tribe's armband and I didn't see wrong," Fargo snapped. "It's damn strange and I wonder what it means."

The mayor rose, his small figure moving to stare out through the window for a moment, his face grave. "There's another wagon train due here this week from east Texas, near Idabel. They sent a letter over a month back telling us when they'd likely be arriving and listing the supplies they'll be wanting. Some wagon trains do that. It avoids delays for them when they get here and lets our merchants have whatever they need waiting for them. But now I'm even more worried about their getting here," he said.

"You could send a search party out to meet them and bring them in," Fargo said.

'The mayor let his ruddy face grow pained. "Red Sand is made up of merchants and some ranchers like Aran, here. I can send our undertaker, Jake, out with a burying party but I don't have the kind of men to send out a squad to escort wagon trains. That'd take a proper patrol of fighting men. The army ought to be doing that."

"The army?" Fargo frowned.

"Yes. They've a permanent field post west of here along Coldwater Creek. They're supposed to patrol and protect the whole region," Gibson said.

"Sounds as though you don't think they are," Fargo observed.

"It's damn plain they're not," the mayor shot back. "Maybe you ought to go tell them what you saw."

Fargo let his lips purse in thought and he saw Jennifer's hazel eyes watching him. "Do that, Fargo. I'll go with you. I'll back up what you say," she said. "God, anything that'll stop another massacre of innocent people."

Fargo thought a moment before answering. "I could give it a try. But there's something I want to do, first," he said.

"Whatever you do I'm sure will help," Aran Tooney said as he pushed himself from his chair. "Meanwhile, I've got to get back to my place. There's work waiting to be done."

"I'll be here for anything I can do, Fargo," the mayor said. "Though I still think you misread some of those markings you saw."

Fargo's smile was a dismissal and he found Jennifer at his side as he walked from the office. She went to the Ovaro with him while Aran Tooney waited in the buckboard. "What are you going to do now?" she asked.

"Go back to where the wagons were hit. I want to have another look around," he said.

"And then?"

"Depends on if I find anything."

"Will you go visit the army field post?" Jennifer asked.

"Yes, I'll do that."

"And then?"

"Go my way. I'm expected up Kansas way. Folks here have to find their own way to battle this," Fargo said.

Jennifer's hand rested against his shirt. "Come by the ranch later. I've things to say to you. Please?" she asked.

"All right," he said and waited until she

stepped into the buckboard and drove away with her uncle. He climbed onto the pinto and rode from town. He followed the road out until he turned up into the hills and finally he neared where the wagons had been attacked. He detoured and made a half-circle to where he had fought off Jennifer's attackers. The three braves had been taken away, he saw. He dismounted to examine the area. But he found nothing to help him and he rode back to where the wagons were — silent, strangely macabre shapes.

He saw the row of narrow mounds, each with a crude cross of branches at the head. The burying party had done its job. But the real monuments were the empty wagons, each a headstone to hopes and dreams brutally shattered forever. He turned north and quickly picked up the wheel marks of the wagon they had used to haul away their stolen bounty. The tracks moved higher into the hills. When he passed through a line of short hawthorns, the tracks disappeared. He halted, frowning as he swept the ground with a long, practiced gaze. He explored to the left, then to the right and finally rode on higher along the hillside. But there were no more wheel tracks. The trail had been obliterated — carefully and thoroughly wiped away.

His lips pulled back in a grimace. It was one

more strange turn, one more departure from what should have been. He was about to turn away when he saw a lone horseman at the crest of the hill, skin glistening bronze in the sun. The rider stayed motionless, watching him and Fargo started the Ovaro up the slope. He kept the horse at a walk and the Indian continued to stay in place. Fargo moved upward at the slow pace, his eyes narrowed as he watched the Indian. He was three-quarters of the remaining distance to the top and the Indian still hadn't moved.

A small, sudden game had blossomed, Fargo realized, a contest of nerves, will and daring. He was close enough to see the Indian's face. It had a broad nose, high forehead, cheekbones prominent but without the flattening common to so many Indians. A Cheyenne face, Fargo decided. The Cheyenne face had its own strong characteristics, a result of their lack of tribal mixing. Out of some thirty individual tribes, only the Arapaho and the Wichita were more fullblooded than the Cheyenne.

Fargo's hand went to his holster as he neared the crest of the hill and the Indian still hadn't moved a muscle. He held a short, powerful bow in his bronze-skinned hands, Fargo saw, but no arrow in place. Fargo found himself wondering at the Indian's game. He drew the Colt, banged the pinto in the ribs with his heels and the horse sprang forward in an instant gallop. The Indian spun his pony and disappeared down the other side of the hill. Fargo kept the Ovaro at a gallop as he reached the crest and charged down after the fleeing Indian. He could see his quarry clearly as the Indian dodged in and around the buckthorns that dotted the slope in small clusters. The Ovaro's powerful strides devoured the downward slope and Fargo was gaining rapidly. He had just swerved past a cluster of buckthorn when he heard the sound that was a half-whistle and half-hiss of air, a sound completely its own. "Shit," he swore aloud as he flung himself forward across the jet-black neck of the Ovaro and felt the two arrows skim his back.

Staying flat, he yanked at the reins and swerved the horse to the left as another arrow whistled past. He swerved right and went into a wide circle as he looked up to see two Indians emerge from the buckthorn. A quick glance below and to his right revealed two more bronzed riders racing into sight while the one he had been chasing had turned and now charged back toward him. Fargo cursed again as he stayed flat against the horse and let the Ovaro's powerful hindquarters drive up the slope. He allowed himself a quick glance, raised his arm, and fired off three shots designed to slow the trio that chased him.

The shots had their effect and he saw the three braves veer away, losing at least thirty precious seconds as they did so. When they brought their ponies back in pursuit, Fargo had reached the top of the hill, twenty seconds translating into forty feet. He charged over the crest and down the other side. He slowed for a moment, half-turned, and raised the Colt to fire, but saw the braves halt atop the crest. Fargo held his fire, the Colt ready to take aim at the first one off the crest. But the Indians as one, turned to disappear down the other side. Fargo sent the Ovaro downward as he kept the Colt in hand and slowed only when he reached the bottom of the slope. He halted, drew a deep breath as he reloaded and cursed his own stupidity. He had let himself be trapped, gone charging after the Indian like a damn schoolboy.

Still cursing at himself, he turned the Ovaro and rode back at a slow trot. He skirted the town and made his way to Aran Tooney's ranch, his first look at the place in daylight. He dismounted a few yards from the main house, and saw a half-dozen ranch hands scattered around the spread, some fixing corral posts, others shoveling manure. Some twenty steers were in the nearest corral and his eyes moved across them. They were thin, too thin to be driven any distance. A few had knee and hock sores that had been painted with iodine. All needed hosing down and a stiff brushing with a long-handled farm brush. Fargo turned away and paused at a line of wagons, unhitched and waiting — three full platform freight wagons with loose canvas piled inside each and two Owensboro mountain wagons with their oversized brakes and reinforced frames.

He turned as he heard the door open and saw Jennifer coming toward him from the house, not wearing her torn brown dress any longer. A white shirt pressed against her full breasts and tan riding britches enclosed long thighs. Her tall frame moved with strength and suppleness, dusty-blond hair flowing out behind her. Only the softness of her hazel eyes contrasted her assured, almost commanding mien. "Why didn't you knock? I didn't know you were here until I happened to look out the window," she said, faint reproof in her tone.

"I was having a look around," he said.

Her smile was chiding. "Fargo, I don't think you ever just look around," she said. "You wanted to get the feel of the place."

"Occupational disease," he said.

"Any conclusions?" Jennifer asked, the smile of quiet amusement now. He thought about his reply for a moment.

"His stock's not in good shape. The place has a run-down feel to it," he answered bluntly, deciding on honesty. "I'm also wondering what brought you out here," he added.

"A visit. Uncle Aran said he wanted to see me," she answered.

"That's nice," Fargo said blandly.

Jennifer allowed a low laugh. "All right, there's more," she said. "But there'll be time to talk about that. What did you find this morning?"

"Something more I don't understand. I tried following the wagon tracks. They were wiped away, not a trace left," he said.

"Why does that surprise you? I thought Indians were masters at hiding tracks." Jennifer frowned.

"Yes, but not that way. There's a fine line of distinction. The Indian knows how to move without leaving a trail. He knows how to use springy grass, flat rocks, water, crevices, every bit of the terrain. He knows how to double-back and leave a false trail. He knows all the ways there are to hide pony tracks. But hiding pony tracks and wiping away wagon tracks are two different things. The last is white man's way."

Jennifer stared back. "You think white men were in that attack? I didn't see any," she said.

44

"Neither did I and I'm not saying there were. I'm just saying this is one more thing that doesn't fit right," Fargo replied.

"You going to visit the army now?" she asked.

He cast a glance at the sky. "Not enough day left. Tomorrow morning," he said.

"I still want to go with you," she said.

"All right, come morning," he agreed. "You said you wanted to talk to me."

"It can wait till morning," she said as Aran Tooney appeared from the barn, gray overalls covering his ample paunch. A figure stepped out from behind him. Fargo took in a woman, not more than thirty-five, he guessed, facial contours unmistakably Indian, black hair worn in two long braids. She was clothed in an Indian deerskin dress, the top cape section cut along the bottom in the uneven pattern of the Arapaho fashion.

"How'd it go today, Fargo?" the man called out.

"Didn't find anything to help," Fargo said as Aran Tooney halted before him, the woman at his side. Her black eyes cast quick glances at him, Fargo noted, uncertain more than shy.

"This is Nako, my companion," Tooney introduced as the woman gave a half-bow. "Found her three years ago at a trading post

45

and decided to take her in. She knew a little English then but I've taught her more since." Fargo's eyes went to Jennifer for an instant and saw she held her face expressionless. "Saw you looking over the wagons," Aran Tooney said. "Guess you're wondering about freight wagons on a cattle ranch."

"It crossed my mind," Fargo said.

"When the cattle business is slow I store the wagons for Joe Odin. He runs a freight line and his place in town is only big enough for one wagon. The storage fee helps pay the feed bills," Aran Tooney said.

"What kind of freight would a man run out of Red Sand?" Fargo frowned.

"Wouldn't know that. I just store his wagons," Jennifer's uncle said. "You'd have to ask Joe."

"I might do that, just to satisfy my curiosity. I'm stopping by to see the mayor," Fargo said.

"Any special reason?" Tooney asked.

"I want to know what more he can tell me about the wagon train due this week before I visit the army."

"You shouldn't be bothering the army," Aran Tooney said and Fargo's brows lifted. "Been talking to folks in town. Most agree with that," Tooney added.

It was Jennifer's voice that cut in. "Why?" she questioned.

46

"It's not the army's business to protect wagon trains," her uncle said.

"It seems to me that's exactly their business," Fargo put in.

"No. Their field post is between the town and a lot of damn savage tribes. They're our protection right where they are. Folks don't want them split up riding guard for wagon trains and leavin' the town unprotected," Aran Tooney said.

"Seems as though they can do both," Fargo said. "I'll talk to them about that."

"I'd say leave things be," the man answered. "You staying in town?"

"Might. I saw an inn there. I might treat myself to a nice soft bed," Fargo said.

"Why not," the man said as he turned away. The Indian woman hurried along with him. "Get supper started," he ordered and the woman left him and headed toward the house as he returned to the barn. Fargo glanced at Jennifer and saw her eyes were narrowed as she stared after her uncle.

"He's so different than I remember him," she said. "But then I haven't seen him in ten years. Now he's somehow harder. And with his Indian woman —"

"A man needs a companion," Fargo said.

"Companion? I'd say slave," Jennifer sniffed.

"You're being harsh again." Fargo smiled.

Her mouth tightened. "You taught me that can be wrong. But sometimes it's the simple truth," she returned.

"Maybe," he conceded. "You said you'd things to talk to me about."

"They can wait till morning," she said.

"I'll be by soon after sun up," he said.

"I'll be ready." She nodded. He climbed onto the Ovaro and watched her return to the house before he rode away, her back straight. Command and assurance were in her every movement, he decided as he turned the pinto down the road toward Red Sand. He reached the town along with the dusk and found the mayor's office dark and closed. He ambled on through town to halt outside a narrow structure with the words ODIN FREIGHT HAULERS painted on the wall. The front door was open and kerosene lamps burned inside. He dismounted, stepped into the warehouse and saw a man with a wheel spoke in one hand. Fairly tall, with a thin face and a thin nose, the man turned sharp blue eyes on him. Straying brown hair that hung low around his head gave his face an added note of scrawniness.

"Looking for Joe Odin," Fargo said.

"You found him," the man answered.

"I was at Aran Tooney's place and saw your

wagons there. Name's Fargo," the Trailsman said.

Joe Odin cast him a frown. "Fargo? You're the one who was at the wagon train," he said.

"News travels fast around here," Fargo commented.

"Hal Gibson called on Jake for a burying party and Jake's a big talker," the man said.

"Seems so," Fargo said. "I was curious about what kind of freight you'd be hauling out of Red Sand."

"All kinds of things. I haul borax sometimes. I ship bolts of cotton fabric brought in from the East. Sometimes I freight wagons of good, rich topsoil into Texas and New Mexico where they've nothin' but thin, sandy soil. Then I haul bags of seed and bales of hay almost to the Mex border where they don't have much of either. I've got regular stops I make," Odin said.

"Interesting. The world is full of surprises," Fargo said.

"Some not so good. I hear you're going to go see the army and try to get them to move against the Indians," Joe Odin said.

"Something wrong with that?" Fargo queried.

"There's a goddamn lot wrong with it. Folks around here don't want the Indians set on the warpath. They'll come raiding and burning and killing," Odin said.

"They're doing that to wagon trains now," Fargo countered.

"Wagon trains are not the whole town. Folks set out in a wagon train, they take their chances. Some get through. Some don't. That doesn't mean you poke a hornet's nest and that's what you'll be doing if you get the army after them," Odin said.

Fargo peered at Joe Odin's face, the scrawniness now turned bitter and dyspeptic. "You ever had any of your freight wagons attacked?" Fargo asked.

"No," the man said.

"That's what this is all about, isn't it? You want the attack on the wagon trains to go on. That keeps the Indians satisfied and they leave your wagons alone," Fargo said.

"I didn't say that," Odin growled.

"You didn't need to. It was plain enough," Fargo said. "Sorry, but I'm talking to the army about their taking some kind of action."

"A lot of folks won't be happy about that, Fargo," Odin called after him as Fargo walked away. Outside, he led the pinto down the darkened streets of town as he let his mind turn over thoughts that crowded each other. He'd had two strong warnings with two different reasons. One came out of fear, the other out of selfishness, but both carried the same message — leave the army out of it. Strange paths that led to strange conclusions, he mused as he reached the center of town and halted outside a small oasis of light, smoky air and the murmur of voices. The sign over the doorway swayed in the night breezes.

"Belles and Bottles," Fargo read aloud as he dropped the reins over the hitching post. There was no better place to sample the mood and flavor of a town than in its saloon, a place where rumor and talk and feelings were all loosened with whiskey. He stepped into the large room and peered through the haze of gray-yellow smoke. A long bar took up one wall, round tables spread across most of the remainder of the room. He counted eight girls moving among the tables, some seated with customers, others idling casually. All were younger than most saloon girls, he noted, and as he halted a woman in a dark green floor-length satin gown came toward him.

She had blond hair on the brassy side but wasn't unattractive despite too much rouge and lipstick. The plunging V-neckline of the dress allowed a view of the curve of long but full breasts. "Hello, handsome," she said, her eyes moving appreciatively across the chiseled strength of his face. "I'm Arlene. I always welcome new customers, especially ones that look like you."

"That's nice," Fargo said blandly.

"What's your pleasure — bottle, belle or both?" The young woman smiled.

"What I really want is some good bourbon and some good talk," Fargo said.

Arlene frowned a moment. "Talk is time and time is money," she said.

"I expect to pay for your time," Fargo said and she moved to a table in a corner of the room with him. Her blue eyes under overly made-up eyelashes studied him for another moment.

"You sure this is all we can do for you, handsome?" she said. "You can talk in bed, too."

"Maybe later," he said and she gave a half-shrug.

"Seems a waste to sit here with somebody looking like you," she said and ordered a glass of bourbon from one of the girls that passed. "What's your name, mister?" she asked.

"Fargo. Skye Fargo," he answered and saw a little furrow come to her brow.

"Heard that name today," she said. "You the one that came onto the wagon train?"

"That's right," Fargo said, pausing to take a sip of the bourbon the waitress brought. "That seems to be the talk of the town."

"Any wagon train massacred is the talk of the town," Arlene said. "Word was that you saved a young woman and killed three Indians. That's sure cause for talk."

"What does the town think about the Indian attacks? You must hear talk about how they feel," Fargo said.

"It bothers the town. Wagon trains are this town's bread and butter," Arlene said.

"How do they feel about the army letting this go on?" Fargo asked.

"I'd say folks don't think there's much the army can do about it," Arlene answered.

"What if the army could do more?" Fargo inquired.

"Such as?"

"Giving wagon trains an escort through the territory, before they reach town and after they leave," Fargo said.

Arlene shrugged. "I guess that'd be fine with most folks," she ventured.

"I was told the town feels that if the army goes escorting wagon trains it'll leave the town unprotected," Fargo slid at her.

She frowned in thought for a moment. "Guess it might," she said. "But I never heard anyone say that."

"That's interesting," Fargo thought aloud. "You hear folks are afraid the Indians will go on the warpath if the army goes after them?"

"I never heard talk of it," Arlene said. Fargo

sat back and finished his bourbon as a wry smile touched his lips. Joe Odin's warning was becoming even more clearly self-motivated. Aran Tooney's warning seemed to reflect his fears more than the town's. Two men, each using the town as an excuse for their own concerns. But just to complete his conclusions, he slid another question at Arlene.

"Any of the army boys ever come here?" he asked.

"Sure, when they get a weekend pass," the young woman said.

"No trouble between them and townsfolk?" Fargo queried.

"Never has been," she said.

"This all seems to mean that the town is satisfied with the way the army's handling things," Fargo said.

"I don't know about satisfied. Everybody'd like to see less Indian attacks," Arlene answered. "I'd say folks are glad to have an army field post in the general area. That's more than a lot of towns have." She sat back and gave him a quizzical glance. "Why all these questions?" she asked.

"I heard things that needed checking out. You've been a help," Fargo told her.

"Now how about my being more of a help? I've some real nice girls," she said.

"This place your own?" he questioned. "Or

are you just managing?"

"It's mine."

"You're young to have your own place," he commented.

"That's because a lot of women start out as bar girls and get their own place after they're worn out. I didn't do that," she said.

"You didn't come up through the ranks," Fargo said and she smiled.

"Exactly. That's a nice way to put it," she said. "But you haven't answered me."

"I'd only be interested in management," he smiled and her eyes narrowed on him for a moment.

"You tempt me to make an exception," she said. "I'd have to think more on it."

"I'll be at the inn," he said, pushing back from the table.

"I'm not saying," Arlene murmured.

"Whatever," he said. "Thanks for the talk." She rose with him, the deep V falling open enough for him to see the side of one lovely curve. He strolled from the saloon and felt her eyes watching him. He smiled as he undid the reins from the hitching post. She would be worth waiting for, he had decided, a definite cut above the usual. But there was more chance that she'd not show. He was aware of that and he pushed her from his mind as he walked back through town to where he had seen the inn near the north end of the main street.

He saw a notice that the kitchen was still open and took the time to eat before he paid for the room on the first floor. He left the light out and undressed to his underdrawers in the faint glow of the moonlight that filtered through a lone window. The room was neat and clean and that was more than enough — a single bed along one wall and a dresser and wash-basin against the other. He stretched out on the bed and his thoughts idled, Joe Odin and Aran Tooney sliding across his mind. Odin was easier to understand. Apparently he was an unscrupulous man, concerned only with his own self. Other people, wagon trains, the town itself, played little or no part in his thoughts. Aran Tooney was harder to decipher.

Was he that afraid for his run-down ranch? Or his own neck? Or was there more? Did he look to the protection of the army because of his Indian companion? Did he feel the tribes would be glad to make him a special target? Some would, Fargo realized. But then, if they wanted to single him out, they could do so any time. The army field camp was miles away. Sometimes fear, especially the very per-sonal kind, can make a man think like a fool.

Fargo closed away his thoughts, rolled on

his side and let himself doze. The night deepened, and he was falling into a sound sleep when he heard the knock at the door. He smiled as he rose, wiping the sleep from his eyes and admitted to some surprise. He'd more or less decided she wouldn't show. The smile still toyed with his lips as he pulled the door open. He had only a split second to see the three figures, all crouched, when the rifle stock smashed into his forehead. He staggered backward, the world spinning away. He managed to half-turn and the second blow from the rifle stock grazed the side of his head. He hit the floor face down and lay still. His gunbelt on the bedpost was too far away to reach. He was dizzy, his vision a blur, but he could hear the voices clearly.

"Get his clothes," the one voice said, a deep, growling sound to it. "You help me carry him out, Jake. Orders are to get rid of him someplace else."

Fargo felt his legs being lifted, then hands closing around his arms. He kept his eyes closed as he was dragged from the room. "Down the backstairs," another voice said. Fargo let himself stay limp as he feigned unconsciousness. He'd find a better moment to make his move. At least he hoped so.

3

Fargo felt himself being carried from the room, two men holding him as they pushed down a few steps and through the rear door. "I'll bring his horse around," he heard the third man say and he lay still on the ground. There was still no way to reach the blade in the calf holster with both figures standing over him. He continued to play unconscious and listened to the sound of the horse being brought to a halt in front of him. He was lifted again and draped across the saddle on his stomach, legs and arms hanging limply on each side of the Ovaro.

His head throbbed fiercely where the rifle stock had smashed into him but he kept himself hanging lifelessly as the horses started to move. Using his ears as eyes, he fixed two of the men riding in front and one staying behind. They moved slowly from the town, staying to the rear of houses. He soon smelled the change in the air as they rode up a low hill where buttercups bloomed. He didn't dare wait much longer, he realized.

They could decide to finish him off at any moment. He began to flex the muscles of his abdomen in and out, and he felt himself begin to slide from the saddle. He stayed limp as he continued to roll his abdomen until suddenly he slid from the saddle. He let himself fall to the ground in a crumpled heap and lay still. "Shit," he heard the rider in the rear spit out and listened to the sound of the man as he dismounted. The other two had halted, also. "Help me get him back up again," the one man growled. But Fargo, in the crumpled position, had one hand down at his calf where, hardly moving a muscle, he drew the thin, double-edged blade from the holster. He felt the two men bend over him, their hands reaching for him.

"Screw it. We finish him off here. This is a good enough spot," Fargo heard the third man call from his horse. The other two were still bent over him, about to lift him onto the saddle again when he felt their hands draw away. They were just about to straighten up when Fargo exploded, his arm shooting up and outward in a slashing arc. He heard the nearest man's choking gurgle as he fell back, clutching at his throat with both hands. But the motion of Fargo's arm never stopped, sweeping out in one continuous arc. Stumbling backward and off-balance, the second man couldn't even lift his arm up as the blade sank deep into his ribs.

He half-turned with a groan of pain as Fargo caught him under the arms and spun him around just as the third man fired from the saddle. Fargo felt the body in front of him shudder with the impact of three bullets. But even as the bullets struck, Fargo yanked the man's gun from its holster. He dropped to one knee, still holding the now limp body in front of him with one arm, and fired at the man on the horse. His first shot missed as the horseman ducked low in the saddle. The man fired again as he wheeled his horse and started to race away. Fargo dropped his lifeless shield, took aim, allowing for the buck of a gun he didn't know, and fired at the figure on the fleeing horse. The first shot was a fraction high. The second one hit its target and the man toppled sideways from the horse, landed hard and lay still.

Fargo pushed to his feet and walked to the prostrate form. He saw his own Colt stuck into the man's belt and pulled it free. The horse had stopped and Fargo strode to the animal and saw his clothes wedged under the saddle horn, his gunbelt slung around the horn itself. He dressed and returned to the man and went through the figure's pockets. Then he did the same with the other two, and found nothing to identify any of the trio. They were drifters, hired for a job. Fargo stepped to the Ovaro and climbed onto the horse, his lips a thin line.

The three had been hired. But by whom? Plainly, by somebody who didn't want him paying a visit to the army. Joe Odin was the first name to erupt in his mind. The man had been the most threatening. He could easily have had time to speak to others in town with the same feelings he had. Fargo grimaced as his thoughts went to Aran Tooney. He didn't want to include Jennifer's uncle, yet he couldn't exclude the man. Tooney had been less threatening than Joe Odin but no less adamant in his views.

Tooney knew he was going to stay at the inn, Fargo remembered, frowning. He, too, would have had plenty of time to hire the three drifters. And Joe Odin could easily have had him watched at the saloon. And there was someone else who knew he was going to the inn, he reminded himself, a young woman in a dark green satin gown. Had she passed that information on to Joe Odin? Or to somebody else? He pushed away further speculation as he unhurriedly made his way back to Red Sand. The saloon was dark and closed when he drew to a halt alongside the building. He glanced up at the second floor and paused for a moment. The windows there were mostly closed and dark also. He dismounted and closed one big hand around the door knob. The lock, a flimsy mechanism, gave way at once and he slipped into the saloon.

His nostrils drew in the air of stale smoke. A hurricane lamp, burning at its lowest, had been placed atop the bar. It afforded enough light for him to see the stairway. He crossed to it, took the steps in long strides and halted when he reached the second floor. He pressed his ear to the first door and carefully opened it to see a room with two beds, a girl asleep in each. He eased the door shut and went on to the next room where he paused, listened and heard the unmistakable sounds of pleasure coming through the closed door. He moved on to the next doorway, listened again and heard only silence. This time he opened the door to see a room with a single young woman curled up asleep on a bed near the window. Once again he went on, carefully opening each door where he heard only silence until finally he was at the last doorway of the corridor.

He listened, then opened the door and saw a room larger than any of the others. A canopied bed was against one wall. The moonlight gave pale illumination but enough to catch the sheen of the brassy blond hair. He crept into the room, closing the door behind him and stepped to the bed to cover her mouth with one hand. Her eyes snapped open, round with surprise and fear. He kept his hand over her mouth, a firm yet gentle pressure. "No yelling," he murmured and she nodded. He drew his hand away and she sat up, a pink nightgown clinging to her breasts.

"Dammit, I never promised I'd come," the young woman said as her eyes gathered resentment.

"True enough," Fargo said.

"Then you've no right to come barging in here," Arlene snapped.

"That depends," Fargo said.

"On what?" she frowned.

"Somebody else came," he said and she stared back. "I'm wondering if they came in your place," he added.

"No, I didn't send them. I didn't send anybody," she protested.

"You tell anybody I'd be at the inn?" Fargo questioned and she shook her head vigorously.

"No, I didn't talk to anybody about you. Honest," she said.

His eyes searched her face. There was an honesty about her and she wasn't bright enough to recover so quickly or be that good an actress. He decided to believe her and took a step back from the bed as she sat up. "What happened?" she asked.

"Three drifters tried to kill me," he answered and she blinked hard at him.

"God, I'm sorry," she murmured. "Why'd anyone want to do that?"

"I don't know," he said. "But I expect I'll be finding out."

"Good luck, big man. Come back when you do, if you're still interested in management only," she said. He nodded and walked from the room, hurried down the steps and out into the night. He walked the Ovaro to the inn, tethered the horse and returned to his room. He undressed once more and stretched out on the bed. He had let himself be careless but then he'd had no real reason to expect anyone but Arlene. It wouldn't happen again, he promised himself grimly as he returned to sleep.

• The morning sun woke him and he washed and had breakfast at the inn — good coffee and sweetrolls. When he finished, he walked the Ovaro through the already bustling town to the mayor's office. Hal Gibson was just unlocking the door and Fargo saw the moment of surprise in the man's face. It was understandable, he told himself, refusing to read

64

things into every fleeting expression. "Good morning," the mayor said as Fargo followed his diminutive figure into the office. "You're here early. Don't tell me you've paid a visit to the army already."

"No, got a few questions for you, first," Fargo said. He sat down with a relaxed smile. He had already decided not to mention the attack upon him. There were strange shadows in the town and he'd wait to learn more before becoming confidential with anyone. "That wagon train that contacted you, the one due here this week, they give you any details on themselves?" he asked.

"Matter of fact they did," Gibson said. "Seven wagons, all families. They wrote they'd be wanting extra clothes for five youngsters, three boys and two girls, from seven to ten years of age. They also mentioned extra blankets for two five-month-old babies. Wagonmaster's a man named Holson. Why do you ask?"

"If I get the army to come look for them I want to be sure we have the right train," Fargo said, paused and phrased the next question carefully. "You figure folks agree the army should move out and escort wagon trains?"

"Don't know. Why?" Gibson asked.

"Just wondered. I heard some talk that folks

might feel the army's role is to protect the town and nothing else," Fargo ventured.

"Some might. I wouldn't know."

"Why not? You're the mayor," Fargo said.

"That means I sign official town papers, hire people like Jake, witness deeds and sometimes settle arguments. That's all it means. This is a funny town. Folks don't talk a lot. Folks know that, sitting where they are, all hell could break loose at any time. They live with that by not thinking too much about it," the mayor said.

Fargo nodded and kept further thoughts to himself. Hal Gibson's reply pretty much echoed the one Arlene had given him. But somebody was thinking hard about the army and the Indians and the wagon trains. He'd already learned that the hard way. He'd pursue that on his own, for now, he decided. He left the little man with a pleasant nod and rode back through Red Sand. He turned onto the road from town and across the low hills to Aran Tooney's place. He found Jennifer waiting in a white shirt and tan riding britches, her tall, slender shapeliness austerely attractive. She swung onto a dark brown mare as he rode up and he saw Aran Tooney come out of the house, the Indian woman with him.

There was no surprise in Tooney's eyes at seeing him, Fargo noted, but the man could be a very controlled customer. Or entirely innocent, Fargo reminded himself. "Still going to go talk to the army, are you?" Tooney grunted and Fargo nodded.

"Just remember what I told you about how a lot of folks feel," Tooney muttered.

"I will," Fargo said as he rode away with Jennifer beside him. The army post was along Coldwater Creek, he'd been told, so he turned south to ride along the creek. "You've things to say," he reminded Jennifer as they rode along the soft ground that bordered the water with black willows offering shade from the hot morning sun.

"I wanted to explain my coming here, for one thing," Jennifer said.

"You did that. Your uncle asked you to come see him for a visit. He arranged everything except you switched plans at the last minute and almost got yourself killed," Fargo said.

"That's not all of it. Uncle Aran had a reason for asking me to visit. He never said it in so many words but we both know it. He wants me to invest money in his ranch," Jennifer said and Fargo felt his brows lift. "You saw that it's pretty run-down," she added and he nodded, his glance moving across her willowy loveliness. "You're surprised," she laughed, taking note of the glance.

"Guess so. You're not the investor type," he said. "Least not the ones I've seen."

"All paunchy gentlemen in fine suits and big cigars, right?" she said.

"And some elderly ladies obviously very well off," he added. "You're too young and pretty."

"When my grandfather died he left a considerable fortune and he left it all to me," Jennifer said. "That's how the money comes to be in my young hands. Needless to say, that's one reason Uncle Aran was so horror-stricken when I told him how I changed to the wagon train instead of sticking to his arrangements for me."

"He saw his bankroll go out the window," Fargo said.

"That's right. Am I being too harsh again?" Jennifer slid at him.

"No, not this time," he laughed.

"I've had countless investment offers since I became a wealthy young woman," Jennifer said. "Turned them all down."

"How come you've come to check out this one?" Fargo asked.

"First, Aran is family. Second, I'd love to own and buy a ranch. I'd love learning all about doing it and making it work," Jennifer said and he heard the rush of enthusiasm in her voice. "But I'd no idea this place was in such a savage territory."

"So wait for the next stage back," Fargo said.

"No, I'd like to make this work. It appeals to me. But I'd also like the land to be safe," she said.

"That's not about to happen any time soon," he grunted.

"How about a little safer? I'd settle for that," Jennifer answered.

"That might be possible," he allowed.

"Which brings me to the second thing I want to talk to you about. You can help make it a little safer. And you could help do something else. There were children on those wagons, taken off for slaves. Maybe you could help get them back."

"That's a damn big maybe," Fargo snorted.

"It's worth the trying. I'll pay you to try to get those children back. You've the special talents that might be able to do it," she said.

"But you haven't even made up your mind if you're going to invest in your uncle's place."

"That's right, I haven't. But that has nothing to do with the children. I have all this money. I'd like to spend a little of it on something worthwhile."

Fargo let himself search her lovely face and saw only directness and sincerity in the hazel eyes. "I'm thinking you might be special enough yourself," he said.

"Then you'll do it," Jennifer said eagerly.

"Slow down, honey. I didn't say that. There may be a lot more here than we know. Something sure as hell doesn't fit right. I want to speak to the army, first," he said and his eyes narrowed as the long line of field tents came into view. "Which I'll be doing in another few minutes," he said, spurring the Ovaro into a trot.

The field post took shape, a typical army installation — tents in rows, horses tethered to one side, supply wagons near the creek bank, carbines stacked in triangles at the front of each tent. Everything neat and in order in spite of it being a simple field post. Sentries held their rifles on him and Jennifer as they slowed to a walk and entered the camp. Fargo's glance found the small tent with the troop flag outside it as he reined to a halt. "Skye Fargo and Jennifer Latham. Come to see your commanding officer," he said to the sentry.

"That'd be Major London," the sentry said and led the visitors to the command tent where he disappeared inside as Fargo and Jennifer dismounted. He returned in a moment and showed the visitors into the tent. Major London stood tall behind a small table with two folding chairs in front of it. A sharply creased uniform and a slightly preemptory manner could be the man's way of countering the youthfulness in his face, Fargo speculated. The major was not over thirty, he guessed.

"Please sit down," Major London said and pulled one of the chairs forward for Jennifer. She smiled as she lowered herself onto the edge and the major turned his eyes on Fargo as a half-smile crept across his face.

"I'm sure you don't remember me, Fargo," he said.

"You're right," Fargo said with a moment of surprise.

"I was standing by when you paid your last visit to General Leeds," the major said. "I was on the general's staff."

"Sherwood Leeds," Fargo echoed. "I sure remember the visit. He turned it around to fit his needs, but then that's pretty much always the way with him."

"Yes, sir. The general's always been a special kind of commander," Major London said. "He spoke a lot about you after your visit, told us a lot of things. He thinks highly of you, Fargo."

"The feeling's mutual," Fargo said.

·"Now, what brings you here with such charming company," the major said. He was relaxing, Fargo saw, feeling less need to be formal.

"Some things I can't explain," Fargo said and saw the major's questioning frown furrow his smooth forehead. "Jennifer was on a wagon train that was attacked, only it wasn't like any Indian attack I've ever seen," Fargo said and proceeded to recount everything that had happened. When he finished, the major had sat down behind the table, the furrow deeper into his brow.

"Damnedest thing I ever heard, Indians stealing sewing machines and tables," London said. "I'd have trouble swallowing it from anyone but you, Fargo."

"You know Mayor Gibson of Red Sand," Fargo said and the major nodded. "He said it's been going on some while. They'd seen evidence of it in other attacks."

"He never said anything to me about it." Major London frowned.

"I think they didn't know what to make of it," Fargo said. "But there's more, maybe worse. I saw one brave with Cheyenne markings on his moccasins, another wearing a Kiowa armband and Wichita designs on another's pouch. Have you seen any signs of the tribes getting together?"

"No, nothing. But the thought scares the hell out of me," the major said. "But that doesn't make sense, either. The tribes stay away from each other except for an occasional coup raid and even that's pretty much stopped. They're all busy doing their own attacks on the white man."

"Who is the largest force in this immediate region?" Fargo questioned.

"The Cheyenne. They have three camps. The major one is up in those hills past the creek, led by a chief named Tallisan. The other two Cheyenne camps are north. The Kiowa and Wichita are both farther south," London said.

Jennifer's voice cut in. "The Indians have been attacking wagon trains. You're aware of that, aren't you?" she asked with a touch of reproof.

"Yes, Miss Latham, we're aware of that," Major London said. "We try to stop them whenever we get the chance but that means our patrols have to be at the right place at the right time."

"Why don't you move against the Cheyenne? If you hit them hard it might put an end to their attacks," Jennifer said. "If you don't move against them, they'll never stop."

Major London turned a pained expression Jennifer's way. "That's right logical, Miss Latham," he said.

"But you haven't done it," Jennifer pressed.

"No, ma'am," the major said.

"I suppose you've good reason for that," Jennifer sniffed and Fargo felt sympathy for the young officer's unhappy grimace.

"Sixty-five good reasons, Miss Latham," the major said.

"Would you care to explain that?" Jennifer said.

"I've sixty-five men in this field post. Five are near retirement or partly disabled. They're assigned to feed and wash the horses, treat injured animals and tend to what in a regular compound would be called stable duty. I've three men who are cooks and cook's helpers. I've two men assigned by training to repair broken equipment from wagon axles to bridles and another two young boys as medical corpsmen. That leaves me fifty-three combat troops. Of those fifty-three, half have never fought Indians." The major paused and his eyes were now hard on Jennifer who, Fargo noted, began to show slight discomfort in her face.

"With these fifty-three men, my orders are to conduct daily patrol activity, engage hostiles if we come upon them and maintain a presence in the area to discourage any direct attacks on Red Sand," the major went on. "The Cheyenne chief has some fifty warriors in his own camp in the hills. Each one is an experienced and ruthless fighter. He could call up another fifty from other camps. There is no way in hell I'm going to mount an attack against the Cheyenne on their home ground. Unless I have a direct order to do so, I'm not leading my men into a slaughter, Miss Latham."

Major London fell silent and sat back in his chair, his young face suddenly looking older. Fargo's eyes went to Jennifer. She sat quietly and looked down at her lap and he saw the faint flush in her cheeks. He said nothing and let her finally break the silence as she lifted her head to look at the young officer. "Thank you for such a thorough explanation," she said, her voice very small.

Fargo smiled inwardly. Apologies can be given obliquely, he realized and he lifted his voice to the major. "We know there's a wagon train due at Red Sand. I'd like to find it before the Cheyenne do," he said. "How about giving me a dozen troopers?"

"I've no problem with that, Fargo," Major London said and got to his feet. "I'll have them ready for you in five minutes."

"Good," Fargo said. "But there's still no explanation for the different tribal markings I saw."

Major London made a face. "I know. I'm hoping you'll come onto something that'll explain them."

"Keep hoping," Fargo grunted as the major hurried from the tent. Jennifer rose and walked outside with Fargo. "We'll talk more while we ride," he said and she nodded and climbed onto the brown mare. Fargo waited until Major London returned with a dozen blue-and-gold uniformed troopers and their mounts walking behind him.

"Sergeant Denton's in charge of the squad," the major said and gestured to a trooper with some years in his face. Fargo nodded at the sergeant as he pulled himself onto the Ovaro. "The squad's with you until you dismiss them, Fargo. Good luck," the major said.

"Much obliged," Fargo said as he wheeled the Ovaro around and set off at a slow trot, Jennifer beside him. The twelve troopers followed in a column of twos, he noted as he turned south back along Coldwater Creek and then headed east.

"The army isn't going to be any help," Jennifer said.

"Seems to be they're riding right behind us," Fargo said.

"I meant in saving the children," Jennifer said. "It's even more up to you, now."

"How so?" Fargo asked.

"The Cheyenne have the children. That's pretty plain. It's also plain that Major London isn't going to go in and save them," she said.

"He's right not to. You heard his reasons," Fargo said.

"Which brings it back to what I said. One man, maybe two, could sneak in and get the children out. That seems the only possible way."

"You're right there," he said. "And wrong at the same time."

"How?"

"Knowing the way to catch a cougar and doing it are two different things," he said.

"You saying it's impossible?" she thrust at him.

"That's not a word I use much, but it's damn close to the truth in this case," Fargo said.

"My offer stands. I'll pay you if you can save those children. A thousand dollars. More if you want," Jennifer said. "It'd make the money I inherited mean something."

He glanced at her. Her hazel eyes were direct as she met his eyes. "That's a powerful lot of money," he said. "But I'd have to be alive to enjoy it." Her lips pressed hard into each other as she looked away, a reluctant concession in the gesture. She fell silent as they rode eastward. They'd gone almost a mile when he put the thoughts circling inside him into words. "You might never settle here and you don't really know those children. Why has this reached so deep inside you?" he asked.

"I don't know," Jennifer said and he saw only honesty in her eyes. "I asked myself that last night. I don't know why it has. I only know that it has. It's as if I feel somehow responsible."

"That's crazy," Fargo said.

"Yes, it is," she agreed. "But it's always been that way with me. I get funny feelings about things and later on I sometimes find out there was a reason. I can't explain why they happen, only that they do. I don't expect you to understand, not when I don't myself."

He smiled inwardly. He knew about feelings that were beyond explaining. Intuition, some called them. A sixth sense, others said. But if you survived in the wild, you knew about the unexplained — knew and listened. Yet Jennifer had hinted at something more, the darker depths beyond intuition. Her voice broke into his thoughts.

"You haven't answered me," she said.

"I'll think more on it. I want to find that wagon train, first," he said. She nodded and rode quietly beside him. Fargo let his mind go back to the events of the night. He purposely hadn't mentioned them to Jennifer. There were still questions he wanted to wrestle with alone and her uncle was part of those questions. Somebody had tried to have him killed.

He'd find out who and why, he promised himself.

Major London had his own reasons not to stir up a hornet's nest, but it was apparent others didn't know that and those others had to include Joe Odin and Aran Tooney. Odin still held first place in his suspicions, Fargo admitted silently. He had accused Odin of being callously content if wagon trains were attacked so long as it satisfied the Cheyenne and they left his freight wagons alone. That uncaring callousness was terrible enough but was it enough to try and have him killed, Fargo wondered. Or was there more? Perhaps Odin had somehow arranged some kind of devil's bargain with the Cheyenne that kept his wagons untouched. The army stepping up activity against the Indians could destroy such an arrangement. That was enough reason to have a man killed, Fargo thought. Then there was Aran Tooney. He had definitely been upset, but his reasons were unclear. Or very well-hidden.

He still couldn't dismiss Aran Tooney but he put the man aside as he wondered if there was someone else, someone among the townspeople. He'd pay another visit to Arlene, he decided, question her again, probe deeper. Perhaps she knew more than she realized. He broke off his thoughts as he saw the road that led to Red Sand and he waved the troop to a halt. "Sergeant, will you have two troopers escort Miss Latham to where she's staying. She'll show them the way," he said.

"What?" he heard Jennifer snap out. "Absolutely not. I'm going along."

He turned a calm gaze her way. "We'll be riding hard from here on. If we find the wagon train we may find the Cheyenne, too. I'll be too busy to keep tabs on you," he said.

"I can keep tabs on myself. I was part of this from the start. I'm going to stay part of it," she said. She reached into her saddlebag and pulled out a Starr six-shot, double-action .44 with a lever rammer under the barrel — a good, fast-shooting revolver. "It was in my trunk when we were attacked," she explained.

"Very nice," Fargo said as he turned away. "Carry on, Sergeant," he said and saw the two soldiers move forward to flank Jennifer on both sides.

"Damn you, Fargo. This isn't right. It's not fair," Jennifer flung at him.

He ignored her and spoke to the two troopers. "You can catch up to us at a gully east of Red Sand," he said and moved the Ovaro forward.

"You won't get away with this, Fargo. It's not fair," she called after him as he rode on. The rest of the troop followed and he glanced back after a moment to see the two soldiers riding away with Jennifer between them. He put the Ovaro into a canter and he skirted Red Sand, moved across a low hill and continued eastward. The land grew harsher, with more pyramids of rock and sandstone formations rising up amid the black oak and buckthorn.

He slowed when he reached the gully east of the town. The trip to Aran Tooney's ranch was not much of a detour and the two troopers were quick to arrive at the gully. "There's a broad passage that runs east from the end of this gully. It's a path a wagon train would be likely to take," he told the sergeant. "Move along it and if you come onto the train, fire a single shot."

"Where will you be?" the sergeant asked.

"I'm going up onto the high land for a better look around," Fargo said. The sergeant nodded and led his squad forward as Fargo turned and rode up the sloping sides of the gully. He sent the Ovaro on across the hilly terrain and up a passage that moved sharply higher. When he was on the high ground, he picked his way between rock pinnacles until he found a ledge that let him look down on the terrain below. Hills, rock formations and heavy foliage allowed only a partial view of the land below. He saw no signs of wagons along

81

the half-dozen logical passages that cut through the land. But the wagon train could have taken a more sheltered route, he realized. He slowly moved the Ovaro down from the high land, riding eastward as he did. His lake-blue eyes searched the terrain on all sides, probing passages first, then halting to listen for the sound of wagons.

He had taken more than an hour to return to the low ground and he rode along a thickly tree-covered stretch of land when he spotted the dozen troopers, the sergeant a few paces ahead of the others. They were almost below him, riding slowly through a ravinelike cut of land bordered on both sides by steep, tree-covered slopes. Fargo's lips pulled back in distaste. The sergeant had led his men into the ravine because he plainly felt it was a route the wagon train might take. But the narrow cut of land was a dangerous place. Fargo swore silently as he watched the troops below. The sergeant was obviously one of the major's men that had never fought the Indians.

Unable to see the end of the cut, Fargo decided to move down the steep side, confident the Ovaro could handle the treacherousness of the slope. He moved along the ledge of land until he was some dozen yards ahead of the troopers in the cut and let the Ovaro begin to pick its way down. He used his weight to help the horse hold its footing, leaned his body to the right or left as he felt the horse balance itself along the steepness. A small rainwater gully of land appeared to afford the pinto an oblique path and a few moments later Fargo emerged at the bottom of the slope just as the troopers came up and drew to a halt.

"Not a sign so far," the sergeant said.

"Didn't see anything, either," Fargo said. "We'll turn north at the end of this cut. They could be above us if they went north along the Cimarron. But mainly I want to get you out of this cut." He turned the pinto around to ride alongside the sergeant when he heard the sudden, sharp half-scream. He spun in the saddle, the Colt in his hand at once, to see the horse and rider a few yards back come half-falling, half-sliding down the steep slope at the other side of the cut. He glimpsed the bounce of dark-blond hair as the horse stumbled, went down on one knee and somehow managed to right itself to slide down to the bottom of the slope.

"Goddamn," Fargo spat out but not just because of the dark-blond form clinging to the brown mare. His eyes had already picked up the other forms that moved through the black oak along the top of the slope, bronze-skinned riders that flicked in and out of the trees. "Run," he shouted. "Everybody flat in the saddle. Get the hell out of this cut." He whirled the Ovaro around and raced back to where the brown mare had just shook herself into controlled footing. "Come on, goddammit," he yelled at Jennifer as he wheeled around again and started after the troopers already galloping full speed. "Flatten down," he threw back at Jennifer as his eyes went to the figures atop the slope.

They wouldn't come down the steep sides, he knew. They'd lose too much time doing that. Almost as if to affirm his thoughts, the first volley of arrows showered down. The Indians raced along the top of the ridge as they fired and another volley of arrows instantly followed the first. Fargo swore as two shafts grazed his shoulder as he lay flattened across the neck of the Ovaro and he glanced back at Jennifer. She was on his heels and trying to stay low, dark-blond hair streaming out behind her. Another shower of arrows filled the air, aimed mostly at the fleeing column of troopers racing just ahead of him. He saw two of the arrows strike, one hitting a trooper in the upper arm, another slamming into a soldier's thigh. Both men clung to their mounts as they streaked forward. The attackers continued to rain arrows down into the ravine but they were hampered by having to shoot through the thick foliage that covered the steep slope.

Thank God for small favors, Fargo muttered to himself as he came abreast of the sergeant and saw the end of the ravine appear some fifty yards ahead. A thick stand of cottonwoods formed the end of the small ravine and beyond the trees, three low hills rose up in step fashion. "Into the cottonwoods and hit the ground," Fargo shouted to the sergeant as he raced past, Jennifer still on his heels. He reached the end of the ravine and saw the high sides of the slope begin to taper down but the troopers had another forty-five precious seconds to get to the cottonwoods. Fargo leaped from the Ovaro as he entered the trees and saw Jennifer almost fall from the mare to land beside him on the ground.

The bronze-skinned attackers charged down from the tapering end of the slope, firing a fusillade of arrows into the trees as they did. Fargo brought the Colt up and fired and one of the racing riders flew from his pony. The troopers, firing from prone positions, brought down four more of the attackers with a strong volley. Fargo saw Jennifer pull the Starr from her waist and get off a shot that went wild. The Indians quickly gave up on another frontal attack. They split their forces into two groups that raced parallel to where the troopers were positioned, firing arrows into the trees as they did. Fargo's quick count showed at least fifteen more of the Indians still attacking and he heard a cry of pain from one of the troopers as an arrow struck home.

Fargo watched three bucks wheel and come charging toward where he lay alongside Jennifer, weaving their ponies as they came. They fired a small cluster of arrows from their short, powerful bows and Fargo cursed as he flung himself to one side as he saw a shaft hurtling directly at him. He felt the feathers of the arrow graze the side of his forehead when he heard Jennifer's short scream. He rolled back onto his side to see that one of the bucks had continued to charge forward and he was leaning from his pony in an effort to grab hold of Jennifer. Her shot went past the Indian's shoulder and Fargo saw the man's hand close around her wrist as he attempted to yank her onto his pony. Fargo fired and the Indian's back arched stiffly as the bullet tore through him. He stayed on his mount for another few seconds before toppling backward to the ground.

Fargo swung the Colt around, but the other two bucks were already racing away. Another volley from the troopers brought down two more of the attackers. Fargo saw the braves wheel and remain in two groups as they broke off the battle and raced away. They rode up into the high ground and disappeared into the trees but Fargo called out in warning. "Stay down," he yelled as his eyes stayed on the trees and his ears listened to the sounds of horses racing through brush. He let another full minute go by before he pushed to his feet. "All right," he said and the troopers began to rise as he reloaded the Colt.

"See to the wounded men," the sergeant called out as Fargo turned to Jennifer, his lips a thin line.

"How the hell did you show up here?" he barked.

"I followed the two troopers after they left me at Uncle Aran's," she said with cool defiance.

"Damn you, girl," Fargo snapped.

"You should be thanking me," Jennifer said and he frowned back. "If I hadn't slipped coming down the slope you wouldn't have looked up and seen the Indians. Their first volley would've hit you."

Fargo glanced at the sergeant as he came up. "She's right about that, sir," the man said.

"That was luck. That doesn't make her right," Fargo snapped and strode away to halt before one of the lifeless Indians. He knelt and studied the armband the man wore — a decorative pattern, boxes and squares in red, green and yellow dye separated by black out-lines. "Cheyenne," he grunted and pushed to his feet.

"Sergeant," he heard one of the troopers call out and he turned to see the man pointing into the distance. Fargo's eyes followed and he saw the long, swooping lazy flight of the birds rise from the other side of the first hill. "Damn," Fargo murmured and felt a knot twist inside him. He saw his feelings reflected in the grim nod the sergeant gave him.

"Mount up," the sergeant called out and Fargo stepped to the Ovaro as the troopers began to remount. Jennifer climbed onto the brown mare as she frowned at him.

"What is it?" she asked.

"Vultures," he muttered and saw her lips tighten. She rode in silence beside him as he led the way up the low hill and down the other side. He saw the wagons only when he reached the bottom of the hill, seven, stretched out in a ragged line. The vultures flew into the air only after Fargo rode into their midst — wide, black wings flapping in annoyance. His eyes moved across the bodies that littered the ground and lay draped half out of the wagons, many gouged and torn by sharp beaks and talons.

"Oh, God," he heard Jennifer gasp and he threw her a quick glance. Her face had drained of color and he saw her swallow hard but she stayed in control of herself, her back held rigid. He dismounted and walked to the wagons where the canvas had been pulled away. Some of the contents of each wagon had been spilled onto the ground, but it was plain that many objects had been carried away. One Conestoga had only sheets and a trunk of clothes left in it, he noted. His eyes went to the ground and the footprints that led away from the wagons. He also saw the long, scraping marks where heavy objects had been dragged.

Jennifer and the sergeant went with him as he followed the marks through low, scraggly brush, uphill, then into a bank of black oak. He halted when he came out the other side of the trees. The terrain here was mostly dirt and rock and the marks had been wiped away. He examined the ground to the right for some dozen yards, then to the left. When he returned to where Jennifer and the sergeant waited there was a grim admiration in his voice. "Wiped clean. Very carefully done. They used branches with leaves. Best brushes in the world. Then they moved on using flat rocks wherever they could," he said.

"I'll get my squad and we'll follow farther," the sergeant said.

"We won't find anything. They've wiped

out their tracks as they went along," Fargo said.

"You still say this isn't the Indian way?" Jennifer queried.

"Not naturally," Fargo answered, turning away and walking back to the wagons, Jennifer following with the sergeant. He was moving slowly down the line of slain and gouged bodies. He fought away the wave of revulsion that welled up inside him as he continued his grim survey. He paused at the smashed bodies of two infants before he turned to Jennifer and the sergeant. "There were children, three boys and two girls, seven to ten years of age. They're not here," he said.

"They were taken," Jennifer breathed and Fargo nodded.

"Goddamn them. And we only got six of the bastards," the sergeant swore.

"The ones that attacked us weren't the ones that hit these wagons," Fargo said and drew glances of surprise.

"Meaning no disrespect, sir, but how in hell do you know that?" the sergeant asked.

"It's called knowing your enemy." Fargo smiled grimly. "These wagons were hit at least five hours ago, maybe more. Indians don't hang around where they've attacked for that long. They strike, finish the job and cut out. Maybe the ones that hit these wagons were Cheyenne, too. I can't answer that. But they weren't the ones that hit us."

"Damn all of them," the sergeant said as he stared at the carnage all around him. "What now? We can't just leave these poor souls to the buzzards. We don't have shovels and it's too far away for them to send a burying party from Red Sand."

"We make do," Fargo said and the others frowned back. "We use the wagons. We un-hitch the horses, then take the wheels off. We use the canvas, gather branches and stones."

"Yes," Jennifer said. "It'll be fitting in its own way. I'll start gathering branches."

The sergeant barked orders to his men and Fargo joined in to unhitch the horses. It took time and the men worked in silence. When it was finished there was little of the day left. But the wagon frames were neatly stacked side by side and thoroughly covered with branches, canvas and stones, a small wood cross mounted on each. He had seen far cruder caskets, Fargo reflected. Jennifer had been right. There was an appropriateness to it.

"We'll take the horses back with us," the sergeant said as he had his troops mount up. "The army can always uses extra horses." Fargo nodded in agreement and Jennifer came up to ride alongside him as he began to lead the way back. He took a path that avoided the ravine. Night fell before they neared Red Sand where the sergeant called a halt. "We'll be going back our way from here," he said. "I'll give Major London a full report."

"Tell him I might be stopping by again," Fargo said and the sergeant turned his horse with a quick salute. Fargo watched the column ride away, the three wounded men flanked by two troopers each. "I'll take you back to your uncle's place," Fargo said to Jennifer without looking at her.

"You going to keep sulking because I didn't stay put?" she tossed at him.

"I don't sulk," Fargo snapped.

"Sure looks that way to me," she returned airily.

"Be quiet and ride," he muttered and put the Ovaro into a trot.

She caught up with him. "Just don't make those children pay because you're mad at me," she said.

He didn't answer but he swore silently at her. She knew how to hit and where, damn her. Thoughts tumbled wildly through his head. He had to sort them out before giving her an answer, any answer. She was asking things she'd no right to ask, not of anyone. Certainly not just to satisfy her own inner feelings. He rode wrapped in his own silence as thoughts continued to whirl inside him. He wouldn't hurry answering. Wouldn't and couldn't.

4

The moon hung high when Fargo rode into Aran Tooney's place with Jennifer and waited while she stabled the mare. The door of the house opened and Aran Tooney stormed outside as Jennifer returned from the stable. "Where the hell have you been?" he thundered at her, his jowly face darkened.

"I told you I was going to visit the army with Fargo," Jennifer said.

"All damn day and half the night?" Tooney returned.

Fargo saw Jennifer's face stiffen. "I don't need a chaperone," she said.

"I'm not being a chaperone. I was worried about you," the man answered.

"We went to look for that wagon train," Jennifer explained, softening her tone.

"You find it?" Tooney asked quickly.

"Too late," Fargo broke in and Aran Tooney's face curled into a pained expression.

"Tough luck," the man said. "Did the army agree to go chasing Indians?"

Fargo chose his words selectively, unwilling to reveal everything the major had explained. "Major London said he'd do the best he can," Fargo answered. "I expect we'll be talking some more."

Aran Tooney's eyes went to Jennifer. "We'll talk in the morning," he said, turned and strode to the house. Fargo caught a glimpse of Tooney's woman companion in the doorway as the man went inside.

"I shouldn't be resentful. I'm sure he's concerned about my safety," Jennifer said.

"For one reason or another," Fargo commented and she offered a half-shrug of wry admission.

"He's concerned. Maybe that's enough. Maybe reasons don't matter. Maybe only actions count," Jennifer said.

Fargo smiled. "Reasons matter, even if it's convenient for you not to think so."

"Perhaps," she conceded. "But right now I'm more interested in actions."

"Actions," he echoed. "Is that another word for answers?"

"I guess so," she said.

"I'll want a night on it," he said. "I'll come by in the morning."

"I'll be waiting," she said and watched him swing onto the pinto and ride away. He took a pathway across a low hill, found a wide-branched box elder and bedded down beside it. He let thoughts slide through him as he lay stretched out on the bedroll. On the surface, it all seemed simple enough: the Indians attacking the wagon trains, the redman striking at the intruders. He yearned to dismiss it as just that but grimaced because he knew that was impossible. There were strange layers just below the surface. Indians making off with pieces of furniture, carefully wiping away trails in the white man's fashion. Perplexing, aberrant behavior. Yet they had taken youngsters, a very normal pattern. Nothing fit. And someone had tried to have him killed to keep him from bringing the army into action.

It would have been unnecessary. Major London had his own good reasons for prudence. Of course, his would-be killers hadn't known that. Or were unwilling to take any chances. Then there was the Cheyenne armband, the Kiowa and Wichita markings. Perhaps signs that were the most ominous of all. He frowned. Layers, all under the surface. Even Jennifer had them, normal feelings of compassion and concern on the surface and underneath, a strange sense of responsibility. But none of it was his concern. He was passing through. He wasn't involved.

He let out a bitter snort as the thought flickered for a moment. But he was involved, of course. He had become so the minute he'd gone to Jennifer's aid that first afternoon. He couldn't have turned away then and he couldn't now. He wouldn't hang high-flown motives on it. Not even conscience. Just the way of the world that pulled a man into things. He turned on his side and drew sleep around him with a grim resignation.

He woke with the new day sun and found a stream large enough to wash in. He breakfasted on wild plums and finally made his way to Aran Tooney's ranch. The man, with a shovel in hand, came toward him as he dismounted. Fargo's eyes were pulled to the side of the stable where two more wagons had joined those he'd seen at his first visit, one a platform-spring grocery wagon with a roof and closed, high-paneled sides. Fargo strolled to it and saw the rear door hanging open. The wagon was empty inside, he noted. But the second wagon was definitely not empty. A light, dead-axle dray with stake sides, it held three rows of steel-banded casks, unmistakable in their appearance.

"Some more of Joe Odin's wagons?" Fargo commented.

"He brought them in last night," Tooney said.

Fargo rested a hand on one of the casks. "A wagonload of whiskey kegs. Strange cargo,

I'd say," he remarked.

"You'd be even more surprised to know where it's going," Aran Tooney said.

"Surprise me," Fargo said.

"It's going to doctors," Aran Tooney said and Fargo's brows lifted.

"Let's have that again," he said.

"To over a dozen little towns in south Texas," Tooney told him. "Chloroform's almost impossible to get. Cocaine's too hard to use, so doctors use whiskey, kegs of it. When they have to take out a bullet or an arrow or operate on a man they knock him out with whiskey. These whiskey kegs are being used for a real good purpose."

Fargo let the explanation hang in his mind. It was not so strange as it might sound to some. He had seen whiskey used as an anesthetic often enough and he let his eyes go to the high-paneled grocery wagon. "What would he be hauling in that?" he asked.

Aran Tooney shrugged. "I'd guess anything that needs to be kept out of the direct sun," he said.

"That makes sense," Fargo agreed.

"I suppose you've come to see Jennifer," Tooney said and Fargo nodded. "She's in the guest room. There's a separate entrance around the other side of the house." Tooney started to walk away and paused to glance back. "You going to be staying around these parts?" he queried.

"Not for long," Fargo answered and the man walked on. Fargo strolled to the far side of the house and saw a door and a small window near it. Jennifer opened the door at his knock and he stepped into a small, neat room with a single bed and a bureau making up the furniture. Jennifer wore a white shirt hanging loose over blue Levis. The hazel eyes searched his face.

"I slept poorly last night," she said. "Waiting can do that."

"Guess so," he said.

A half-pout touched her usually coolly composed features. "You going to make me ask?" she pushed at him.

He drew a deep breath. "Only for the children," he said and she frowned back. "I'll go look for them. I'll see if I can find them. That's all for now."

"Then we've a deal. I can pay you now if you like," Jennifer said.

"No deal, no money. My treat," Fargo said.

Her hazel eyes probed his. "Why?" she asked.

"Sometimes you do things for money. Sometimes you do them for yourself," he answered. She continued to study him, her smooth brow furrowed. "It's not because I've any strange, damn fool feelings inside," he added.

"I told you, I don't understand them but they always mean something," she said, a sudden burst of frustrated anger filling her voice.

"No matter, really. I'll be going now," Fargo said. She came forward in a quick motion and her lips were against his, sweet softness and just the points of her breasts touching his chest. She let him answer, open his mouth on hers and he felt the moment's touch of her tongue before she pulled back. "Promises?" he asked.

"No, no promises," she said.

"What, then?"

She thought for a moment. "Admissions," she said.

"I'll settle for that." He smiled. "For now."

"I want to go with you," she said and his eyes answered. "I was a part of it from the start. You can't just shut me out."

"Maybe another time. Right now my only chance to get close is alone," he said.

"When will you come back?" Jennifer asked.

"I don't know," he said.

"How long before I let worry change into despair?" she asked.

"Patience is a virtue, honey," he said. She

put her lips to his again, quick sweetness this time.

"Be careful," she said and walked outside with him, watching him leave from the doorway. He waved back as he turned the Ovaro south. He swung west along Coldwater Creek and it was late afternoon when he sat in the command tent across from Major London.

"That's right, straight over the hills. The rest is heavy forest," the major said and sat back in the thin chair to fasten Fargo with a narrowed glance. "You know, Fargo, the Cheyenne catch sight of you and it'll be your last visit anywhere," he said.

"That's for damn sure," Fargo agreed.

"What if you see the children there? How do you expect to get out one kid much less eight?" the major questioned.

"Haven't thought that far yet. One step at a time," Fargo said as he rose to his feet.

The major's eyes stayed narrowed on him. "Why do I think you'll come visiting again?" he remarked.

"You're lonely," Fargo said, grinning as he strode from the tent. He rode through the lowering dusk as he crossed the hills and he reached the heavy tree cover on the other side as darkness descended. A moon rose to filter a weak light through the thick foliage and he let the pinto slowly pick its way forward until he halted at a spot with a thick bed of star moss. He stretched out on his bedroll, undressed and thought of the major's question. It had been all too accurate. Finding the children was one thing. Rescuing them was another. He let thoughts drift through his mind until he finally slipped into sleep, the question very much unanswered.

When morning came, he moved deeper into the forest with careful deliberateness, walking the horse slowly as he scanned the ground. The grass was too thick and too fresh to show old hoofprints. It wasn't until the morning was nearing an end that he found what he sought: a narrow path worn through the forest, the ground well covered with unshod pony prints in the bare soil. It was a path they rode single file, he noted as he swung onto it, certain the forest held numerous ones similar to it. The passage trailed off finally, the dense tree cover of box elder, black oak and cottonwoods growing lighter, and open land spreading out on the left and right. Pony prints disappeared only with the narrow passage but he saw the bruised lower branches of the trees where the riders scattered to move freely through the woods.

He rode slowly, his gaze sweeping the terrain ahead through the trees and he stopped often to let his nostrils draw in deep draughts of air. The odor was faint but he picked it up, wood fires burning. But any trapper could have a wood fire going. He moved forward a dozen yards and drew in air again. Wood fire and the scent of fish oil and berries. He followed his nose and soon he drew in the scent of hides drying in the sun. He found a spot under a wide-branched cottonwood, sank down against the base of the tree and let himself nap until night fell. When he woke and moved forward under a filtered moon, he led the Ovaro behind him. The odor of firewood and drying hides grew stronger.

The soft glow of fire spread out ahead of him and he tied the reins up the low branch of a black oak and crept forward. The Cheyenne camp began to take shape, in a large ragged oval. He dropped onto his stomach and began to crawl forward. The Cheyenne had no sentries posted, he saw as he drew closer to the camp. They obviously didn't fear a lone intruder and were certain they'd hear a force of any dangerous size. No overconfidence, he grunted. They were absolutely right. But there were always exceptions. He'd try to be one of them, he muttered silently. The tree cover held up almost to the very edge of the camp and Fargo let his gaze slowly travel across the collection of tepees, drying frames, campfires and dried hides stacked together.

He saw pits dug into the ground for cooking, small clouds of steam rising from some where hot rocks had been put into water.

It was a full-scale camp at the end of the supper hour and he watched bare-breasted squaws, some old and thin, some thick around the waist and a half-dozen young girls with lithe bodies. Some of the squaws wore the typical elkskin clothing but in the Cheyenne fashion of a skirt and cape instead of the one-piece garment of so many other tribes. He let his gaze carefully move across the braves, most young, most wearing little beyond breechclouts, wrist gauntlets, armbands and moccasins. But the only markings he saw anywhere were Cheyenne markings and those included the decorations on the tepees. As he lay prone, his eyes shifting back and forth across the camp, he saw the flap of the largest tepee come open and a man emerged, his flowing black hair hanging around a strong face — high cheekboned with eyes having a slight Oriental cast.

The man wore two eagle's feathers in his hair and a breastplate of bone strips that covered his chest down to the waistline. The nearest braves respectfully stepped back and the squaws offered quick bows. *Tallisan,* Fargo murmured silently. The chief stepped forward, took a bowl of food offered by one of the squaws and sat down in front of the fire to eat. Fargo saw the tent flap pulled open again on the large tepee and a young woman emerged. An elkskin dress, fancily decorated, hung loose over a body that nonetheless offered long curves of thigh and hip and breasts that pushed the fabric of the garment outward. The firelight caught her face and Fargo saw beautifully even features, high cheekbones and skin smooth as a hazel nut, a straight nose and full lips. Jet-black eyes danced in the firelight as she knelt beside the chief.

The chief had an eye for beauty, Fargo reflected. He took his eyes from the girl and slowly swept the camp again. The children he sought were nowhere to be seen. His gaze lingered on each tepee. None had extra guards outside it. There was nothing unusual in the camp. Perhaps they had already put the children away for the night, he murmured to himself. He watched the chief rise and return inside his tepee. The young woman followed him and pulled the tent flap closed after her.

Fargo continued to watch the camp, his eyes going to every brave or squaw that entered or left a tepee. Finally, the camp settled down for the night, most of the women inside the tepees while a good number of the braves slept outside on blankets. Fargo swore silently as he crawled backward and halted under a black oak where the underbrush grew high. He'd have to wait till morning and hope they didn't send out an early hunting party that might come upon him. He settled down, removed his gunbelt and put it next to him so he could stretch out in comfort. He let sleep come on the soft night breeze and woke only when the morning sun slid its way through the trees.

He strapped his gunbelt back on and began to crawl forward again. The Cheyenne camp was waking when he halted between two cottonwoods and he saw the tall figure of the chief standing outside his tepee. Tallisan had exchanged the breastplate of bone strips for a short calfskin vest embroidered with beadwork. Fargo's eyes moved slowly across the camp as more figures emerged from the tepees, but he saw no captive children brought out. He watched the squaws carefully as the camp breakfasted on fruits. None brought food or water into any of the tepees and as the sun rose over the top of the hills he saw a half-dozen braves gather their bows and quivers. They were preparing to ride out, probably to hunt game. But they would spot the Ovaro, Fargo realized grimly. Luck wasn't running his way at the moment.

He swore softly and began to crawl backward, forcing himself to stay low and silent. He didn't push to his feet until he was out of sight of the camp and then he ran through the brush to where he'd left the horse. He flipped the reins from the tree branch and swung into the saddle in one quick motion. The Cheyenne hunting party could be on its way, he realized and he swung the horse to the right and rode deeper into the trees. He'd give them a chance to pass rather than have them come up on his tail, he decided. He pulled to a halt, his ears straining for the sounds of horses moving through the woods.

The sound came to him in minutes, the Cheyenne moving swiftly with easy confidence, making no effort to be quiet. He waited until the sounds faded away and then began to make his way down the hillside. He took a long curve to stay away from the hunting party and the sun was in the midday sky when he crossed over the last hill and rode onto the flatland. Major London's neat and ordered field camp came into sight in another hour and the sentries watched him ride in without halting him. The major stepped from the tent as Fargo rode to a halt.

"No luck," he said, reading the grimness in the big man's face.

"The children aren't in that camp. There wasn't one sign of them," Fargo said. "I got close enough to see everything."

"Strange," the major murmured.

"Everything's strange about this thing," Fargo said.

"You looked. You risked your neck to do that. There's nothing more you can do," the major said. "Maybe they were sold off already."

"Indians don't sell off slaves that quickly, especially young ones. They'd keep them for a while at least. Maybe I looked in the wrong place. You said there were other Cheyenne camps to the north."

"There are," the major said.

"Then there are the Kiowa and Wichita to the south," Fargo said. "The children were taken. They've got to be someplace."

"The Cheyenne camp you went to is the closest, the biggest and the most logical one to have them," the major said.

"So much for logic," Fargo snapped.

"Good God, man, you've come back. You were lucky. You try going to every other camp and you can be sure your luck will run out," Major London said.

Fargo swore inwardly. The major's words were too damn true, he realized. "I'll think some more on it," he allowed. "I'll come visit again."

"I expect you will," Major London said

with a hint of wryness in his voice and offered a salute as the big man rode away on the Ovaro. Fargo followed Coldwater Creek once again, east this time, halting once to let the horse drink and rest. Night blanketed the land when he reached Aran Tooney's place. The ranchhouse was dark and he saw the wagonload of whiskey kegs were still there along with the others. He drew up to the side door where a light was on in the adjoining window. The door opened quickly to his soft knock and Jennifer stared at him, her eyes wide and round as they searched his face. She wore a pink shawl over a pink nightgown.

"You didn't find them," she said as he stepped into the room.

He frowned back. More than a guess. More than reading his face. She could have drawn many answers from that. The inner sense she'd told him about was there. "They weren't there. I've no answer. I expected they'd be there," he said. "I'll look some more."

"Other Indian camps?" she queried.

"If I have to," he said.

She frowned into space for a moment. "No," she said with quiet firmness. "You've done enough. I can't ask any more of you."

"My treat. I told you that," he said.

"My conscience," she returned. "I did the urging."

109

"You were so damn concerned about the children. You going to just give up like that?" he tossed back.

"I guess I'll have to," she said.

"What about that strange inner responsibility? That all go away?" Fargo pressed.

"No, dammit. That's still there but I'm not adding you to it," she almost shouted. He saw her fists clench, knuckles white. Her lower lip quivered but there were no tears, only bitter despair. He took her by the shoulders, turned her to him.

"I'll make a deal for now. I won't go searching the other camps. I'll just go back looking more or less where I was. I know the terrain there now," he said.

"What do you expect to find you didn't find before?" she questioned.

"I don't know. Maybe the children aren't being held in the main camp. I don't know why in hell they wouldn't be but it's worth looking around some more," he said.

She said nothing for a long moment. "Maybe. I don't know what's right anymore," she answered finally.

His hands moved and the shawl fell from her and he closed his fingers around very round, very smooth shoulders. The nightgown dipped at the neck and he saw the rise of lovely twin mounds as her bare arms lifted, encircled his neck. His lips found hers, pressed and she gave a tiny moan as her mouth half opened, worked against his and then she tore away. "What happened to admissions?" he asked.

"Nothing. I'm just not ready for more than that," she said. "I have to be sure."

"Of what?" he asked with more irritation than he'd intended. But the hazel eyes were wide and full of sincerity, he saw.

"I need to know it'll be as special to you as it would be to me," she said. "That I wouldn't be just a casual, passing moment." Fargo winced inwardly. He'd heard similar words before. They always spelled trouble. But his eyes were fastened at the front of the nightgown where the two tiny pink points pressed against the lace of the silk, barely visible yet all the more exciting because of it. What the hell, he thought. Loveliness was always worth a little extra trouble.

"It'll be special," he said, his voice soft. She followed his eyes, scooped the shawl up and cloaked herself with it. Her hand rested on his chest.

"Give me a little more time," Jennifer said. "I want the wanting to carry away everything else, for both of us."

He wanted to say he was ready to be carried away now but he held the words back. "Of course," he said soothingly and Jennifer's lips held his again for a brief, warm kiss. Only a day ago he had told her that patience was a virtue. He repeated the same words to himself now. But it was also a pain in the ass, he added as she walked to the door with him.

"Be careful," she said as he climbed onto the Ovaro.

"Always," he said and rode away quickly. Jennifer was a sincere young woman. She took life seriously, even the strange inner feelings she could neither explain nor understand. Yet she was no fool. She had seen through Aran Tooney's concern for her. A strange combination of astuteness and naïveté, he decided as he rode into the hills, found a spot to bed down and quickly stretched out on his bedroll. Pleasant wonderings about Jennifer brought sleep quickly and the night stayed warm and still.

5

A breakfast of good apples — crisp, bright-red Winesaps — and water from a cold stream, sent him on his way with the early morning sun already turning hot. He rode along Coldwater Creek but skirted the field command post as he climbed the hills beyond it. He refrained from moving into the thick forest as he drew near to the Cheyenne camp and rode to the west where the tree cover lessened and the hills became rockier. He rode slowly, scanning trees and ground, picked up old unshod pony prints as the soil grew grassy, but he saw nothing that would indicate a side camp.

An outcrop of red clay rocks appeared, a stream tumbling down their steps to form a freshwater pond. He edged the Ovaro underneath the shade of a big post oak as he caught the sound of voices. He saw the figures appear moments later, a half-dozen squaws, most very young and among them the young woman he had seen with the Cheyenne chief. She led the others to the pond and he noticed they stepped back deferentially to her as she knelt down at the water's edge.

Her jet-black hair hung loosely and she was every bit as lovely as when he'd first seen her, her features, prominent yet delicate, giving her face a dusky classical beauty. With a sudden movement of her arms, she whisked the elkskin dress off and stepped into the pond. Fargo felt the sharp intake of his breath at the beauty of her. Slender, her waist narrow, her legs long and lithe, she paused ankle deep in the water and lifted her face to the sun. Beautifully curved breasts, full and firm, were each topped by a soft brown nipple and a flat abdomen led down to a tiny little triangle of jet-black curls. She immersed herself in the pond for a brief instant and then rose again to face the sun, her red-brown skin glistening with tiny beads of water. She was shimmering loveliness and his eyes were fastened on her as the other young girls began to shed their garments.

The six horsemen that appeared over the crest of rock behind the pond wrenched his eyes from the Indian girl. The young bucks were all near naked. As he watched, they charged down toward the pond. He saw the girl spin in surprise and look at the intruders. One buck raced his pony directly toward her — a well-built figure, handsome except for a cruel slash of a mouth. The girl stepped from the pond, scooped up her dress and started to run up along the stepping-stone rocks. But the young buck was close behind her, his pony sure-footed on the rock. Fargo saw him reach down and seize the girl by her flowing jet hair. She let out a scream of pain as he yanked her back.

Fargo pulled the big Sharps from its saddle case, lifted the rifle and fired. The shot was too hasty and sent a spray of rock chips flying into the air as it struck just behind the Indian. The girl pulled free as the brave spun around in surprise. He ducked low on his pony as Fargo fired again, backing the horse down as he clung to the far side. Fargo saw the girl running up the rocks, trying to reach a high ledge. With a quick glimpse, he saw the other bucks stop chasing after the other maidens as his rifle shots exploded. The powerfully built buck had disappeared behind the stepping-stone rocks but Fargo heard the pony racing upward. Fargo pushed the rifle back into its saddlecase as he sent the Ovaro racing from beneath the tree. He was high enough to reach the crest of the rocks first and he was waiting there when the girl appeared, the Colt in his hand.

She had pulled the elkskin dress on as she'd run and her black eyes widened in surprise as she saw him and came to a stop. She half-turned as the young buck came up behind her from the other side of the rocks. He saw Fargo and again dived low across the top of his pony as Fargo fired. He was fast and the shot missed. Hanging onto the pony's mane, he slid himself under the horse's belly as he turned the animal around and raced down the passage. Fargo glimpsed his moccasins touching the ground as he hung beneath the horse. They had Cheyenne markings.

Fargo rode the Ovaro toward the girl and she watched him come without flinching, her black eyes boring into him. She was uncertain of him but she was also unafraid. He reached a hand down to her. She paused a split second then grasped his fingers and let him pull her onto the saddle in front of him. "He will come after you again with the others," she said and Fargo nodded. The Cheyenne spoke mostly the Algonkian tongue and while he was most familiar with the Siouan language, he knew enough of the other to get along. And the Cheyenne were masters of sign language.

He swung the Ovaro around and crossed the ledge of rock as he saw the buck reappear, the others at his heels this time. Fargo swerved into a thin line of hackberry, reined to a halt and leaped to the ground. "Stay," he said to the girl and emphasized the command with a gesture and she nodded. He dropped to the ground on one knee as the buck spied the Ovaro and headed for the horse, the others spreading out on both sides of him. Two of them partially blocked a clear shot at the lead brave but they'd serve equally well as targets. He fired twice and both the Indians fell from their ponies at once, almost as though they had been rehearsing it. Fargo saw the others instantly break the charge and wheel away. He fired another shot and saw it hit one of the Indians in the arm but the buck stayed on his pony as he raced behind a rock.

They had taken cover but Fargo knew it would only be for a moment. Yet he didn't need much more than that and he flung himself onto the Ovaro behind the Indian girl and sent the horse racing through the hackberry. He had spotted a hillside bare of trees when he'd searched the terrain. He raced for it as he heard the ponies coming in pursuit of him again. The girl clung to the Ovaro with easy grace, her back braced against his chest with a muscled firmness. He reached the edge of the open hillside with his pursuers still coming after him, but now he could let the Ovaro full out. The horse charged down the open ground with all the power and speed in its magnificent body. He felt the Ovaro's enjoyment of the run.

The short-legged Indian ponies quickly fell behind and they were only halfway down the hillside when Fargo charged into the trees at the bottom. He drew to a halt, leaped to the ground and yanked the Sharps out again. He was on one knee, the rifle raised as the young buck reined up and motioned to the others. He was smart, Fargo conceded, aware he'd be an easy target on the open hillside if he continued the pursuit. Fargo fired off a shot as the four Indians raced back up the hillside, more of a gesture than anything else. He watched as the attackers reached the top of the open hillside and disappeared into the hackberry. He rose and reloaded the rifle before returning it to the saddlecase. The young woman gazed down at him from the saddle, her high breasts pushing the top of the elkskin dress out.

She looked down at him regally, mingled with an edge of apprehension. "Thank you," she said. "Why do you save an Indian girl?" she asked.

He shrugged. "Indian girl. White girl. Same thing," he said. "You were being attacked."

"You speak our tongue," she said.

"A little. I speak Sioux better," he said.

Her black eyes appraised him and he saw her face soften. "You are very different," she said. "A very great warrior."

"You are very beautiful," he answered with a smile. Only her eyes smiled back. "I saw you at the camp," he said and she couldn't hide the surprise that came into her face. "You were with the chief, Tallisan," he said.

"My father," she said simply and it was his turn to be surprised. "You were spying on the camp," she said.

"Yes," he admitted. "I was looking for someone."

"Who are you?" she asked.

"I am called Fargo," he said.

"Fargo," she repeated very properly, turning the name in her mind. "I am Sunrise," she said, using sign language to make certain he understood.

"We'll go carefully the long way," Fargo said as he pulled himself onto the horse. "Maybe we can find your friends."

"They have gone, run back to the camp," she said.

"Who was he?" Fargo asked. "Why did he come after you?"

"He is called Broken Knife," she said, answering only one part of his question. She fell silent and he saw she wasn't about to answer the second part. "What will you do with me?" she asked after a few minutes. She turned to look at him, her black eyes searching his face and he knew what thoughts raced through her mind. She wondered whether she had avoided one captor only to find herself worse off.

"Are you afraid?" he asked.

She didn't answer for a moment. "I don't know," she said finally.

"But you were afraid of Broken Knife," Fargo said.

"Yes," she nodded.

"I'll take you close enough to your camp so you can go back alone in safety," he told her.

"Take me to my father," she said and her smile was almost mischievous as she saw his moment of hesitation. "Are you afraid?" she asked, turning around his question to her.

"Not afraid. Not sure," he said.

"My father will see you as a brave warrior who fought off Broken Knife and five of his men to save me," she said. "Take me into camp."

Fargo let the thought hang in his mind for a moment. There'd be a risk. Maybe the chief wouldn't be happy with his daughter or him. Yet it would let him have a thorough look at the camp, even if the chief's cooperation was limited to polite gratitude. "All right," he said and her smile took on a note of quiet triumph. She was used to having her way. He moved the Ovaro forward through the trees and she sat relaxed in the saddle in front of him. His eyes swept the woodland as he rode, alert for a reappearance of angry, near-naked figures. But there were none and he proceeded deeper into the forest.

It was when he turned on a direct line toward the camp that he suddenly heard the pounding of horses' hooves and the leaves quivered in a wide line in front of him. He drew the Colt, held it in one hand hidden against the Indian girl's hips as the riders appeared. They stretched out in front of him, riding hard. They pulled their ponies to a sudden and surprised halt as they spotted him. They converged at once, eyes on the chief's daughter in the saddle with him. She sat very straight and held up one hand, a quick, imperious gesture. The Cheyenne warriors swung in on both sides of the Ovaro.

Sunrise cast a glance at the warriors as she spoke to Fargo. "They were on their way to search for me," she said and reached her hand back to where the Colt rested against one side of her firm, small rear. "Put away," she said.

"No, thanks, honey," Fargo muttered and she cast him a glance of annoyance but drew her hand away. He kept the pinto at a walk as the Cheyenne stayed alongside him, each face a stern, cold visage. The camp came into sight and some of the braves rode on ahead and when Fargo entered the camp with the girl he saw the Indian chief waiting. Fargo drew to a halt in front of the man who, he saw, had his bone-strip breastplate on again. Sunrise slid to the ground as Fargo dismounted and she spewed words at her father too quickly for him to understand. When she finished, the chief eyed the big man in front of him with a steely glance. He took a step forward finally, and made the sign language gesture for thanks.

"He can speak our tongue some," Sunrise said and the chief inclined his head to one side as he continued to study the figure that stood tall in front of him.

"You fought off six warriors to save my daughter and you have spied on our camp, she tells me," Tallisan said, his voice deep and gravelly. "Bravery and cunning are the marks of a great warrior." Fargo offered a half-bow for the compliment. "Why did you spy on our camp?" Tallisan asked.

"I search for children taken from a wagon train after an attack," Fargo said.

"They are not here," Tallisan said. "You are free to look in every tepee."

Fargo believed the Cheyenne. The man would not give him permission to search if he had the children. "I take the great chief's word," he said, cloaking the answer in courtesy and respect.

Tallisan showed satisfaction in his face. "I

have taken slaves. I will take them again. What you have done for my daughter stands alone. I will honor you and only you for it," he said and Fargo nodded in understanding. The Cheyenne chief was making it plain that an individual act would change neither attitude nor actions of the deeper, larger picture. "Darkness is almost with us. You will eat with us and stay the night," Tallisan said.

"Whatever the great chief wishes," Fargo said. He wanted the man relaxed, willing to perhaps offer information.

Tallisan turned to those looking on, barked commands and a young girl came forward. Taller and larger in build than Sunrise, a little on the chubbier side, she had a round face that was young and not unattractive. "Mikoma is yours," the chief said. "You may have her for the night or take her with you."

To refuse would be an insult, Fargo knew. The gift was a handsome one in Cheyenne eyes. He was being offered a tribal maiden. "The great chief is generous," he said and his glance went to Sunrise. Her handsome, even-featured face was mostly expressionless but he thought he detected the hint of displeasure in her eyes as they met his. As dusk began to quickly slide into dark, the fires were made brighter and Tallisan gestured for Fargo to join him at the edge of one blaze.

Fargo lowered himself to the ground across from the chief. Sunrise sat to one side and he caught her glance. Her eyes offered the hint of a private exchange. Two squaws brought wooden bowls of semi-soft food that tasted of camass root and tepary beans. "I would not sit beside you for this meal, my father, except for Fargo," Sunrise said. Fargo felt the moment of surprise shoot through him. The statement had been made openly, in front of him, with almost an edge of reproach in it. She was out to make a point cloaked in private meaning.

"Mikoma is a great enough gift," the chief said between mouthfuls, not looking at his daughter.

"I have said the great chief is generous," Fargo put in, unsure what was expected of him.

"You have spoken. I have spoken," Tallisan said with firmness and Fargo saw Sunrise concentrate on her bowl of food with the kind of silence that was not really silence. She had a lot of rebel in her, Fargo decided. The heritage of being a chief's daughter.

"I would ask questions," Fargo said with proper politeness. The chief's nod was permission. "Some of those who struck the wagon trains have worn Kiowa markings and Wichita paint and Cheyenne marks. I have seen this myself. What does this mean?" Fargo questioned.

"The Cheyenne have joined no one," Tallisan said, his voice growing cold.

"Have the tribes joined together?" Fargo pressed.

"The Cheyenne have joined no one," Tallisan repeated and now his gravelly voice had grown sullen. Fargo decided to try a different tack.

"The man who tried to take Sunrise was a Cheyenne," Fargo said.

"He is not a Cheyenne," the chief snapped.

"His moccasins wore Cheyenne markings," Fargo insisted.

"Did you hear my voice? He is not a Cheyenne," Tallisan said, his face darkening. Fargo was grateful to the two squaws who interrupted with pieces of hot venison. The chief bit into his piece with more than irritation. Fargo ate and stayed silent. A glance at Sunrise saw a tiny smile touch the corners of her lips as she ate. She was enjoying the said and the unsaid, it was obvious. Fargo continued to stay silent and let the chief's anger wear away. "We share the skill of our hunters with you," the Cheyenne said to Fargo, a boastfulness in his voice. "Can the blue-coat soldiers hunt so well?"

Fargo smiled. The Cheyenne was canny,

the question really designed to find out how close he was to the army. "I know nothing of the soldiers," Fargo said. "I search alone for the stolen children." The Indian grunted and continued eating and Fargo sorted out words for his question. "Tallisan is the chief of the Cheyenne. He knows many things. Does he know who has taken the children?" he asked.

The Indian's face stayed impassive as he finished his venison without a reply. Finally, he answered, not looking at his questioner. "I will think," he said and rose to his feet, his legs unfolding with smooth power. Fargo rose at once, too. "Until the new sun," Tallisan said and Fargo nodded.

"I will take Fargo to the tepee," Sunrise said.

"The old squaws will take him," her father said firmly. He raised his voice in a command and two withered, bony squaws came forward. Tallisan turned and stepped into his tepee while Sunrise lingered for a moment more.

"Mikoma will come to you when the moon is high," she said. "You can rest first."

"I don't need to rest," Fargo said and the Indian girl's black eyes held a veiled smile. She turned away and disappeared into the tepee. Fargo followed the two old squaws to a small tent at the very end of the camp. They went inside with him and one lit the tallow in a small, stone bowl. The interior of the tepee instantly glowed with a dim light, enough for Fargo to see Indian blankets and mats thrown carelessly on the ground that served as the floor of the tent. The two old squaws withdrew in silence and Fargo removed his gunbelt, undressed to almost nothing and stretched out on the blanket. The Cheyenne chief had made it plain that he was being treated with respect only because of what he had done. Honor dictated that much. But honor did not dictate more than that. Respect was a statement, not an embrace.

Tallisan had his own integrity and he had no intention of compromising that. He had made it plain that enemies were still enemies. But he was also holding something back. The questions had angered him, Fargo reflected. Anger that was a cloak. But for what? Something that concerned only him and Sunrise? Or did he know about the stolen children? And of the strangeness of the attacks? What was the Cheyenne chief hiding? The questions danced a grim rigadoon through Fargo's mind and the final question danced the hardest. Would he have any answers before he left in the morning?

He pushed aside the thoughts and closed his eyes. He let himself doze until he woke with the sound of the tent flap opening. He pushed up on both elbows and saw the Indian girl enter the tepee, a half-smile on her face of uncertainty and shyness. She halted before him, but he saw her eyes move over his smoothly muscled body. With a quick motion, she whisked the deerskin garment over her head to stand naked before him. She had a large-framed figure with young, smooth skin and a little padding over the hips, almost baby fat. Those hips and legs would be heavy in a few years. But her breasts, small for her frame, were still tight and firm and he watched her take two steps and drop to her knees beside him.

She offered a shy smile as her hands began to slide across his chest and down along the sides of his body, a warm touch, not without sensitivity. He lay back, half-closed his eyes, curious as to what she would do next. He heard her soft breathing as her hands moved down his chest, slid over his hard abdomen. He suddenly felt her body moving against his, the small breasts pressing into his chest as she started to lay atop him. Her hands were just pushing against his underdrawers when a voice cut into the sounds of her breathing and he heard Cheyenne words, delivered with staccato sharpness. He sat up and astonishment flooded through him as he saw Sunrise at the edge of the blanket. She snapped out words again and Mikoma pushed away from him, scooped up her dress and ran from the tent.

He sat up straighter as Sunrise knelt on the blanket, her handsome face unsmiling. "Why have you come here?" he asked.

"My father did not do me honor. It is for me to be here, not her. That is the right way," Sunrise said.

"He couldn't bring himself to do that," Fargo said.

"He was wrong. It was my decision to make. It was for him to ask me," she said.

"Why didn't he?" Fargo asked.

She made a tiny sound of derision. "His way of punishing me for going so far away from the camp."

"So you are here to defy him," Fargo said.

"I am here because it is my right to be here if I wish," she said haughtily.

"Any other reason?" he asked. She paused and her smile was slow and slightly sly. "Sunrise wonders about the white man," he said.

"Sunrise wonders about *this* white man," she conceded. She raised her arms and pulled off the elkskin dress. The soft light danced on unblemished red-brown skin and beautifully curved breasts standing firm. Her lithe, strong body moved gracefully as she slid forward — her waist narrow, especially for an Indian girl, legs firm and muscled yet very female. He reached out, closed his hands around the red-brown shoulders and pulled her to him and she came without protest, her legs stretching out as she lay down beside him. He smelled the sweet odor of wintergreen oil as she came against him.

He pushed down the remainder of his underclothes. She lay tight against him and he enjoyed the silken-smooth touch of her. Her black eyes searched his face, no fear in them, only an eager intensity and he pressed his mouth to hers. Her response was tentative and he slid his tongue out, pressing her lips open. His hand slid down to curl around one silky red-brown breast and she gave a low, murmured sound. He moved his mouth down to the pink-brown tip, caressed it gently with his tongue. The murmured sound became a soft, cooing moan — a sound he had never heard before. He continued to caress her nipple with his tongue, drawing more of the red-brown breast into his mouth and enjoying the firmness of it. The soft moans stretched into one long sound.

His mouth stayed on her breast as he let his hand trace its smoldering trail down her body and felt her palms press harder against his back. The moan became a steady, murmured sound, rising up and down within a small range, always low, always soft. His hand lingered across her flat abdomen, moved down to the tiny nap. No firm wiriness to it but instead a half-silken quality and the little pubic mound stayed small and soft. His fingers dipped lower and he felt her legs fall open and the low murmur rose, but only in intensity, not in pitch. He touched and felt a moistness beginning. He moved inward gently with his hand. Sunrise responded, her hips half-rotating, responding, and the moistness increased.

She was small, he noticed, yet very soft. Her lithe red-brown legs stretched out, lifted, came together and fell apart, the flesh giving its own answer, the sign language of true universality. He moved atop her, his own flesh throbbingly ready and he slid forward slowly, gently and found the small passage easily embracing him. The Indian girl's moaning, cooing sounds became an unending paean of murmured pleasure. Her flat belly lifted with his sliding motions and joined him in a slow rhythm. He drew his lips from her breasts to look at her. She smiled, her mouth open and consummate pleasure lit her handsome face.

He felt her hand on the back of his neck press his face down into the lovely, firm breasts and he obeyed. She slid her hips back and forth with him and the cooing sounds continued. Her warm thighs were lifted and pressed against his sides and he began to increase speed. She stayed with him, the natural rhythm of her dictating her reply with the ease of nature, not practice. She was tight around him. His pleasure intensified and he felt himself rising, nearing climax. He thrust more quickly and suddenly her legs fell open and the cooing sound stopped. Gasped words he did not know escaped from her lips. Her mouth was open, her black eyes staring at him with ebony fire. Suddenly she was nodding, her head bobbing up and down against the blanket.

He exploded and she came with him, the quick contractions around him proof, the sudden slamming of her legs against his ribs a confirmation and her bobbing head a furious motion now. He held deep inside her, joining ecstacies, the pleasure that knew nothing but itself. Her lithe body was tense against his, her arms clutched around his waist and finally she fell back with a small, hissing gasp. He slowly slid from her and she moved, brought her smooth skin atop him as he lay back. One leg lifted to lay across his groin. He met the black eyes as they bored into his, but he was unable to see behind their veil. She was examining him from her own past. He saw evaluation, appraisal, uncertainty mirrored in her face.

Her slow smile was approval and appreciation, compliments of both the flesh and the spirit that needed no words.

She slid herself up with a determined little motion until her warm, silky-smooth breasts lay against his chest. Her one arm came up and encircled his neck as, head on his chest, she closed her eyes. In moments, he heard the even sound of her breath as she slept and he swore silently. He hadn't been prepared for this. He'd things to ask her and he felt a definite amount of uneasiness. But the night had time enough in it and he put his head back and let himself doze with her. He guessed he had dozed for more than an hour when he woke to the feel of a soft touch at his groin. He glanced down the length of his body. Sunrise was still alongside him but her hands were stroking, caressing and he felt himself responding at once to the softness of her touch.

He pushed up on one elbow and she lifted her handsome face to his, jet-black hair swinging as she leaned her head to one side. Her smile held the soul of the eternal invitation and her hand kept caressing and touching. He saw her glance down at his response and her eyes were moist with wanting when she glanced up at him. Her hands came around to pull at his buttocks as she wiggled onto her back and he came with her. More moistness this time. That was the first thing he felt. And more eagerness as her hips lifted. He came to her and once again the strange cooing sound welled up from inside her.

This time, when she neared the moment of climax, her arms wrapped tightly around him and her legs lifted to clasp his hips and he smiled. The flesh imparts its own wisdoms. The road to pleasure is traveled more from the inside than from the outside. She came with him and the cooing sounds were more urgent without losing their distinctive character. Her ecstacy was not less, he decided, but contained within the self-discipline of her heritage. When it was past that glorious peak, she lay against him again, her black eyes boring into him. She put her head down atop his chest and he gently lifted her face to his.

"No sleeping. It'll be dawn in another hour," he said and used the sign language for the rising of the sun. She sat up, the lovely red-brown breasts swaying gently and he had to force his hands to stay at his sides. "What would your father do if he knew you were here?" he asked.

"He would kill you. Perhaps me, too," she said.

"He would kill his own daughter?" Fargo frowned.

"For disobeying him," she said matter-offactly and Fargo swore inwardly and she was glad she hadn't mentioned the fact earlier. It would probably have had a chilling effect on his lovemaking.

"You came anyway, knowing this?" Fargo questioned and realized the surprise he felt.

"It was safe. He had some peyote. He will sleep till morning," she said.

"Was it worth it?" he asked and then rephrased the question so she could understand it better. "Is Sunrise happy she came to visit?" he asked.

"Yes," she nodded and her smile was quick, her handsome face finding a new warmth.

"What if Mikoma tells how you sent her away?" Fargo asked, suddenly afraid for her safety.

The smile she returned was both superior and chiding. "She will not tell. It would mean her death, also," she said.

He nodded and moved away from the workings of a culture he could barely understand. "Come morning will Tallisan answer any of the questions I asked?" he slid at her.

"No," she said. "I will answer those I can for you." She moved her legs to sit crosslegged beside him, blithely unaware of the strain she was putting on his self-discipline.

"Your father said that Broken Knife is not a

Cheyenne. Was he speaking the truth?" Fargo questioned.

"The truth as it is for him," Sunrise answered. "Broken Knife was banished from the tribe. To my father he is no longer a Cheyenne." Fargo nodded at the logic that followed its own reasoning.

"Why was he banished?" Fargo asked.

"He tried to become chief of the Cheyenne and failed. He fled after that and he was banished." Fargo smiled inwardly. It had been a palace revolution that failed.

"But he hasn't fled far," Fargo mentioned.

"Others such as he came to join him — men banished by the Kiowa, the Wichita, the Comanche and the Apache. Some brought followers, some their women," Sunrise said.

Fargo sorted her words in his mind. Broken Knife had put together a band of renegades. They must be the ones doing most of the attacks on wagon trains. That explained the different tribal markings he had seen. It also meant that the renegades held the children, probably to sell them off as slaves. It was plain that Broken Knife was building a following to establish himself to try again one day to take over as Cheyenne chief.

"Where is their camp?" Fargo asked.

"No one knows. Broken Knife is cunning.

He moves his camp every few days," Sunrise said.

"How many warriors does he have?" Fargo pressed.

"No one knows. My father has heard of others that were banished from the Kiowa and Apache and who brought followers. I know he has guessed that Broken Knife has twenty-five warriors."

"Three less," Fargo grunted, thinking back to his first brush with the renegades. But the three he killed could have been replaced. Renegade bands had a way of drawing dissatisfied converts, he realized. Sunrise interrupted his reflections as she stood up, beautiful and warm and filled with a new controlled sensuousness that was in her eyes and in the way she looked at him.

"I must go," she said as she drew the elkskin dress over herself. He rose as she stood waiting, little-girl-like, until his lips pressed her mouth once again. "I am happy I came to Fargo," she murmured. "Maybe there will be another time and another place." He nodded and she slipped from the tent. Both knew her words were little more than an empty hope, more a testimony to what had been than to what might come.

He lay back on the blanket, closed his eyes and let sleep come quickly. He woke when the sun funnelled down from the smoke hole at the top of the tent, dressed and went outside. He washed with three silent, grim-faced braves in a small stream behind the camp. When he finished, he accepted fruit and some kind of berry cake from one of the squaws. He saddled the Ovaro. As he finished tightening the cinch, Tallisan stepped from his tepee. The Cheyenne chief's face was impassive Fargo noted as he confronted him.

"Mikoma?" Tallisan asked.

"The night was gift enough," Fargo said. "I have no room for a wife now." The Cheyenne nodded, the answer acceptable. "The great Chief Tallisan has an answer to my question?" Fargo asked.

"I do not know who has taken the children," the chief said and Fargo smiled inwardly. The Cheyenne did not know, not with certainty, and he was unwilling to say more. Broken Knife was an outcast and a renegade but the white man was an enemy. Fargo swung onto the Ovaro. He nodded to the chief and slowly rode out of the hostile, silent camp. He had been rewarded for his actions. Honor had been served. The honeymoon, if one could call it that, was definitely over and Fargo hurried the pinto through the forest. The sun grew hotter as he rose into high land and he hadn't slept that much during the night.

When he spotted a broad-branched box elder he halted, dismounted and stretched out on a bed of broom moss. He slept with memories of the Indian maiden he knew he'd not quickly forget — her lovemaking as different as she was.

The sun was past the noon mark when he woke and took to the saddle again. He rode slowly, his eyes surveying the ground as he did. One thing was certain: Broken Knife and his renegade band were not that far away. The Indian operated in the area, moving his camp from place to place but all inside the region where he could easily strike at the wagon trains. Fargo halted on a ledge and let his eyes mark the area into four quarters. He'd systematically search each one, but first he had to pay Major London a visit before the day ended. He sent the horse down the thickly forested hills. He reached the low ground as the day was sliding toward an end and put the pinto into a fast canter until the field command post came into sight. Dusk had come when he sat across from Major London and told him what he had learned about the renegade band.

"That explains the different tribal markings. It doesn't explain carrying off furniture. That still doesn't fit anywhere," the major said.

"You're right. I don't figure that yet," Fargo nodded. "But I'm going to try and find them and the children they took."

"You want a squad of troopers?" the major offered.

"Thanks, but they'd see a squad and disappear. This is a job for one man," Fargo said.

"That's probably the only chance of finding them," the officer agreed.

"When I find them, I'll figure out a way to get word to you," Fargo said.

"I'll come charging. Count on it," Major London said. "It won't be attacking the full Cheyenne camp."

Fargo rose at his handshake and rode from the field camp. The night had descended and he stayed alongside Coldwater Creek until he neared Red Sand. Then he veered away and rode into the low hill country. The moon was moving toward a midnight sky when he reached Aran Tooney's place. He saw the lamplight still on in Jennifer's room and swung to the ground. The door opened at his knock and she was against him instantly, a brief but fervent hug. Then she drew him into the room.

"Did you find them?" she asked.

"Not yet but I was inside the Cheyenne camp," he said.

"Inside?" she echoed, hazel eyes wide.

"Tell me everything. But first, are you hungry? I've some beef left. I can make you a sandwich."

"With some coffee," he said, suddenly realizing that he was indeed hungry. The stuffed chair felt good as he lowered himself into it and began his story to Jennifer with the rescue of Sunrise. He recounted his taking the Indian girl back to the Cheyenne camp and the gratefulness of her father that had let him have free run of the camp. "The children weren't there," he told Jennifer. But from there he put the answer Sunrise had given him into her father's mouth. He finished the story and the coffee and sandwich at the same time.

"So now you'll try to find this renegade and hope the children are still with him," she said.

"I suspect he hasn't sold them off this fast, if that's what he plans on doing. He may just keep them for his own camp. Though I don't think so," Fargo pondered aloud.

"Why not?" Jennifer questioned.

"He hasn't a base camp. He's always on the move. He's not ready to drag slave children around with him. He expects to sell them off," Fargo answered. He rose and stepped to where Jennifer was cleaning the tin plate, encircling her waist with both hands. "I'm glad to be back," he said softly and she turned, her arms sliding around his neck. But her kiss was quick and she stepped back. "Thought maybe you'd be ready to turn admissions into actions," he said.

Her eyes probed his. "I can't help wondering about something," she said.

"Such as?" he returned.

"I've always heard that the Indian way of showing gratitude is the gift of one of their maidens as a reward," she slid at him.

Fargo sorted words in his mind. "It's a custom," he conceded.

"I've always heard it was custom common to all tribes," Jennifer pressed.

"Nothing is common to all tribes," Fargo said and Jennifer waited. "Some offer maidens, some a fine pony," he added.

Her face remained set. "What did the Cheyenne chief offer you?" she asked evenly.

"He offered me a maiden to take as a wife," Fargo said. "I told him I'd no room for a wife," he added, the answer not a complete untruth, he told himself.

Jennifer's face relaxed after a moment and she leaned her head against his chest. "I'm very tired. Will you come back tomorrow night?" she asked.

"Maybe. Depends," he said.

"Tomorrow night, the next night, whenever. Promise," she said.

He nodded. Jennifer wasn't the kind to push. He had concluded that long back. She was filled with her own inner conflicts. They pulled on her. She had to be left to come to awakenings in her own way and her own time. "Promise," he echoed. "That's a word I put store in," he added.

"You can," she said and nodded vigorously. He turned and strode from the house. She watched from the doorway as he rode away. When he was out of sight of the ranch, he cut across a low hill and found a spot to bed down. He fell asleep quickly, very much aware that the days ahead could bring disappointment at the least, sudden death at the most.

6

The sun burned and he was grateful for the thick foliage of the forestland as he slowly crossed and criss-crossed the first quarter-section of land he had marked in his mind. He found evidence of a camp, remains of a fire, unshod pony prints, but the campers had moved away through thick forest terrain that left no tracks. But when he found two more old sites he knew he was making progress. The renegade leader was indeed cunning and cautious but he left marks for those who could read them. Fargo half-smiled as he studied the ground at still another campsite.

They had stayed at least four days at the site, Fargo determined. The condition of the soil around the spot where fires had been built revealed the passing of time. The depth of prints where the horses had been tethered in one spot were a confirmation. He found food remains for more than a single night's encampment. Four days, he murmured to himself, and then the renegade leader moved on.

He was in the second quarter-section he'd marked out for himself when he came upon another abandoned site just as the day was beginning to wind to an end. He found tracks that led east but he knew there was not enough light left to follow very far.

Marking the spot in his mind, he turned and rode from the hills. He cut across thick low terrain and found a shorter passage to the bottom land where he could ride toward Aran Tooney's ranch. Night had come down to blanket the land when he reached Tooney's place and reined to a halt as he saw Aran Tooney's paunchy form crossing the front yard. Fargo dismounted as Tooney halted and Fargo's glance swept the fence where the paneled grocery wagon had been. It was gone, as were the four Owensboro freight wagons. Only the big dray with its load of whiskey remained.

"I see Joe Odin went off with his wagons," Fargo said. "Not all by himself, I'm sure."

"He had a crew of ten, two men to a wagon," Tooney said.

"Two men on the grocery wagon, also?" Fargo frowned.

"That's right," Tooney said. "Joe likes a full crew. Jennifer tells me you have a lead on finding those kids, something about a band of renegades."

"Yes," Fargo said.

"That's real encouraging. Anything more on it?" Tooney questioned.

"Not yet," Fargo answered.

"Keep after them," Tooney said as he strode to the house. Fargo led the Ovaro to the stable, unsaddled the horse and gave him a feedbag of fresh oats. He walked to the door of Jennifer's room and she quickly answered at his knock, clothed in a pink, floor-length housecoat with buttons down the front. The garment sheathed her willowy figure.

"Surprised?" Fargo asked.

"No, but you weren't sure. I didn't let myself hope," she said as she closed the door after him.

"Your word was promise. I told you I put a lot of store in that word," he said and he saw the moment of uncertainty in the hazel eyes before she looked away. He reached out, turned her face back to his.

"I don't want you to be disappointed," she said and he searched her eyes and saw no coyness, only a sincerity tinged with alarm.

"I don't expect to be," he said and brought his mouth to hers. She held back a moment before her lips softened, beginning to respond. They opened and she gave a tiny gasp as his tongue touched hers. He lifted her up, swung her in a half-circle and put her down on the bed against the wall. He opened the top two buttons of the housecoat and she lay watching him with her eyes wide. He halted, shed his gunbelt and shirt and reached down again, this time opening the next dozen buttons of the garment. The narrow opening widened and he saw the edges of both breasts. She lay motionless, her eyes on him but a faint flush had come into her face.

He straightened for a moment, shed the rest of his clothes, aware that his own excitement had already made flesh respond and he felt the warmth surging through his loins. He heard Jennifer's short gasp and then he was kneeling before her on the bed, undoing the remainder of the buttons. He pulled the housecoat from her and she looked back, still motionless but now beautifully naked — breasts longish but well-cupped, a long, lovely line to each. A tiny, very pink nipple topped each breast and his eyes moved down across her narrow waist, flat abdomen and down to the surprisingly thick, almost puffy little triangle. Below it, her legs were held together but the beauty of their long leanness was still very much there.

He moved down, gently lowering himself half-over her and heard her cry out at the touch of skin on skin. He felt the shudder of pleasure and excitement course through her.

He kissed her again, harder, his tongue darting now, caressing, a messenger of greater pleasures. As his hand cupped her breast, Jennifer cried out and half-jumped in his arms. "Ah, ah, God," she said and put her head back, lovely long neck arching as his lips moved down to her breasts. He took one tiny pink tip, passed his tongue back and forth over it and felt it grow firm though remaining small. "Jesus, oh, my, oh, oh my . . . aaaaaah," Jennifer murmured as his mouth gently pulled on each breast, sucking and caressing. Her hands pressed into his back.

He paused to look at her and the hazel eyes were wide, staring with a mixture of alarm and desire. But her lips were open and they made little sucking noises, beckoning to him. Her hand rose to push his head down onto the white mounds again. "Aaaaiiiiii," she cried out and he felt her legs straighten and her body quiver. He let his hand explore an incandescent trail down her body, pause at the tiny indentation to circle it and move down over the flat abdomen. "Oh, oh, oh no, no . . . oooooh," Jennifer cried out as his hand crept to the edge of the black triangle. But her body gave lie to her words as he felt her torso move and her legs draw up. He touched, pressed, found a surprisingly fibril delicacy to the puffy triangle and his fingers caressed, explored and felt her pubic mound rise up.

"Oh, good God, oh, oh . . . oh, yes," Jennifer murmured and he let his hand slip lower, push against the thighs still tightly held together and felt the sudden moistness of her skin. "Oh, God," she gasped out as she let her thighs relax and he pushed his hand between their lean smoothness, cupped the dark, moist portal. Jennifer screamed, a sudden sound, protest and desire mixed in it. He paused, held her and the scream became a soft murmuring. Her thighs relaxed more, fell away and he pushed gently, a probing touch against the wetness of the maiden lips. "God, oh, God," Jennifer gasped. "Oh, yes, yes, oh, yes. Go on, go on."

Her hips were moving suddenly, from side to side, a half-wild, rolling motion and he calmed her sudden frenzy with his arm. He gently probed deeper, feeling the tightness of her slowly give way and heard the groan inside her cries. But her hips continued to move and when he suddenly plunged deeper, the scream tore from her in a wild burst of pure pleasure. He brought his pulsating warmth to her now flowing wetness and she half-screamed again, the scream spiraling as he touched, sliding forward. He came over her, slid in slowly, gently and the tightness held to him. Suddenly she pushed her hips upward, ramming up and forward as if to cast aside his gentleness.

A sharp moment of pain edged her scream but it vanished in the gasped ecstacy as she lifted again. He moved harder, quicker and Jennifer's head fell from side to side against the bed. He saw her hands clutch at the sheet, pulling it up into tiny knots as her body worked with his. "Yes, yes, oh, my God, my God, my God . . . oh, yes, please, please, oh yes," Jennifer cried out, words running together without end, carried on breathy gasps. Suddenly her arms came up, encircled his neck and pulled his mouth down to her breasts even as her torso twisted and surged and twisted again as though she wanted to take more than mere flesh could take.

He felt her stiffen suddenly, the half-screamed gasps changing to an almost silent hiss. Her hazel eyes grew wide and stared at him with a kind of disbelief as the moment of moments swept over her. He let himself explode with her and her scream reverberated against the walls of the room — a piercing cry of ecstacy achieved, heights never reached before, sensations that swept away everything but their own supreme victory. Her fingers were digging into his back as she held in mid-air, her entire willowy body quivering, until the eternity that was but a brief moment ended like the burst of a roman candle.

Her cry was filled with despair as she went limp and he heard the harsh sound of her breath as she gulped in air. He lay with her and her arms encircled his neck as she held him tight to her, his face against the soft long curves of her breasts, one pink tip pressed against his lips. "Oh, Fargo . . . Fargo . . ." she whispered and turned to press her lips against his earlobe. "I'd no idea it could be this wonderful."

"I'd no idea you were so new at it," he said.

She shrugged, the gesture an admission. "I'm glad I waited for the right moment," she said, shifting onto her back and letting a dreamy little smile come to her lips. "I'm glad for something else," she said.

"What's that?"

"I'm glad I could come to you. I never could have if you'd accepted the chief's offer of that maiden as a wife. Aren't you glad you turned it down?" she murmured.

"Definitely. I was just thinking the same thing," he said and her smile took on a hint of smugness as she curled against him. It was there again, that combination of very female urges and little-girl naïveté. But he had returned for more than her promise. She'd made another offer, almost a demand, and he was going to take her up on it. He'd let that wait for morning, he decided as he closed his eyes and slept with her tight against him.

Jennifer slept soundly through the night to wake only when morning came and he slid from her side. She sat up, longish breasts swaying in unison as she rubbed sleep from her eyes and he had to force himself not to return to bed. "I'll dress and saddle the horses while you get ready," he said.

She pulled her hands from her eyes. "The horses?"

"You said you didn't want to sit around waiting. I'm taking you up on that," he answered. Jennifer leaped from the bed into his arms in one bound, all soft and lovely nakedness. He pushed her away and was grateful for the washbasin of cold water into which he plunged his face. "I'll tell you the rest later," he said as he finished washing and threw on his clothes. He hurried to the stable and had both the Ovaro and a horse for Jennifer saddled when she arrived dressed in a dark green shirt and gray riding britches. Her face glowed with an excitement that was not all of the moment.

"It's later," she said.

"If I find the renegade camp and they have the children, I'll have to keep watch in case they decide to break camp again. Or maybe move on completely. I'll need somebody to go to Major London and bring him back," he said.

"Me," Jennifer said and he nodded.

"You can say no. I'll understand. It could be your last good deed if things go wrong," he said.

"You didn't say no," she returned.

"My own decision. I want to do it," he said.

"I have to do it," she said simply.

"Inside feelings again? Those intuitions?"

"Not intuitions. They're simple. They warn you something's going to happen. This is a kind of shapeless fear. It's feeling guilty without knowing why or what or anything at all. It's just there, simmering inside you. I'm sure there's a name for it someplace," she said, her voice made up of half-anger and half-frustration.

"Leave a note for Aran," he said. "Tell him you've gone to town. I don't want anyone looking for you." She nodded and hurried from the stable. He climbed into the saddle and was waiting with both horses as Jennifer returned from the main house. She climbed onto the second horse and pulled alongside him as he rode away. He saw that the big dray piled high with whiskey casks was still in place as he rode from the ranch with the new sun just beginning to edge the hills. Perhaps Odin made a special trip with that, Fargo reasoned as he turned north and elected to climb the steep hills. It was a direction harder on horse and rider but shorter than following Coldwater Creek. When they reached the high hills he called a halt to rest the horses. He sat down against a black oak, his knees drawn up and a furrow running across his brow.

"What are you thinking?" Jennifer questioned.

"I was wondering about Joe Odin. He and his crew go off with their wagons and a band of renegade killers attack wagon trains, take slaves and strange booty and don't seem to bother them," Fargo said.

"You think there's a connection?" Jennifer frowned.

"I can't make one," he admitted. "But I keep wondering." He grimaced, rose and pulled her to her feet. "Wondering's not going to get us anywhere. Let's ride," he said. Jennifer stayed beside him as he swung north and finally found another spot where the renegades had camped. He felt the ground again and made a face. "They left here almost a week ago," he said and began to move north again. They were in high hill country, heavily forested terrain and he had almost ceased searching for evidence of encampments. The land was too dense for that. His eyes searched the forest for any openings that stayed open and formed a passageway through.

The day had gone into mid-afternoon when he found one and steered toward it to suddenly rein to a halt, his eyes riveted on wagon tracks that stretched through the woods. He dismounted at once and let his hands read the earth. The tracks were not more than twenty-four hours old, the edges still soft and pressing in to the touch. "They hit another wagon train and take one of the wagons?" Jennifer asked.

Fargo's eyes narrowed. "Don't think so. More than one wagon made these tracks, but they were traveling single file," he said as he swung back onto the pinto and put one finger to his lips. Jennifer stayed silent, a half-pace at his heels as he followed the wagon tracks. The passageway through the forest left barely enough room for the tracks and he saw where wagons had broken off low tree branches as they brushed past. But the thickness of the forest began to lessen, the terrain still heavily wooded but not so dense. The wagon tracks continued in single file, he observed and he suddenly reined to a halt. He took in a deep draught of air and made a face. He thought his nostrils had picked up cooking fire smoke but he couldn't be certain. He swung to the ground and motioned for Jennifer to do the same.

He dropped the Ovaro's reins over a low branch and Jennifer laid hers alongside and followed at his heels as he beckoned to her. He moved in a half-crouch, nose drawing in odors, eyes sweeping the forest. He halted again suddenly, drew in another deep breath and tapped the side of his nose as he turned to the left. He saw the wagon tracks make a slow circle in the same direction but he no longer followed their marks as he moved slowly through the trees. He halted after another few minutes and now the scent was unmistakable. A bank of cottonwoods rose up in front of him and he huddled close to Jennifer.

"They're on the other side of those cottonwoods. You stay here," he said and saw the protest come into her eyes. "I'm an old hand at this. You're not," he said and she nodded. He lowered himself to the ground and began to crawl forward on his stomach, his lake-blue eyes sweeping the terrain in front of him and to each side. He inched forward through the cottonwoods. There were no sentries, but he hadn't really expected there would be. He wasn't about to take chances, either. Shapes came into sight through the trees and he heard voices. No tepees, he noted, and then felt the frown dig deep into his brow.

He stared at the semicircle of wagons, the big Owensboro freight wagons that had been stored at Aran Tooney's ranch now being loaded by Indians with lamps, tables, chairs, sewing machines and a variety of other household items. He moved his gaze left, through the camp and saw the crew of drivers helping the Indians load the wagons. At the right edge of the semicircle he saw the high-paneled grocery wagon. Not far from the wagon, bound to stakes in the ground, he saw the youngsters and with a quick count he came up with eight. They were all there. It became plain now that they were to be transported in the closed panel grocery wagon, hidden from passing eyes. Fargo's gaze swept the scene again. Joe Odin wasn't with his men. Perhaps he was due to come along later. One thing was clear. The renegades were hitting the wagon trains for Joe Odin. He obviously gave orders as to what to take. He had the means to sell off the stolen objects.

The children were something else. Maybe he had a channel to sell them off, too. Or maybe he was going to sell them off for the renegades, payment for their cooperation. It was probably a tenuous pact but a grisly one — a devil's pact with some of the items still to be filled in. But first, it had to be stopped. He watched the men as they loaded the wagons. There was no hurry. They weren't rushing to leave before night. They'd probably take off come morning, he guessed. But nothing was certain and he started to slither backward, turning on his stomach. There was perhaps two hours of daylight left, he noted with a quick glance skyward, just enough for Jennifer to be well on her way to reaching the field post. He forced himself to stay crawling along the ground until he spied Jennifer waiting and he pushed to his feet.

The question hung in her eyes. "They're all there," he said. "So are Odin's wagons. I won't have the whole picture till it's over. I don't expect they'll be leaving till morning but I'm not going to take any chances. I'll stay and watch."

"Time for me to fetch Major London," Jennifer said.

"He's been alerted he might get some kind of word from me," Fargo told her. "Tell him there are a little over twenty renegades and ten of Odin's crew. I expect he'll bring a full platoon." She nodded and he walked back to where they had left the horses and she climbed into the saddle, her face grave.

"All I have to do is find the way back here," she said grimly.

"Listen carefully. I was checking out the terrain while we rode. You go back to where there's a row of black oak opposite a row of buckthorns. You go between them. It'll be a long trail and the moon will be up when you get to the end of it. You'll see three big cottonwoods in a semicircle. That's your second mark. Go west from there. Your third mark will be the pond where we stopped. Pass to the left of it and swing north till you see a tall slab of granite, some fifteen feet high. Turn due south when you reach it, cut down two hills and you'll reach the field camp. You just reverse things on your way back with the platoon."

"Got it," Jennifer said.

"When you get back to where we are now, the major can come charging. There'll be no way he can sneak up with a full platoon," Fargo said. "The children are tied to stakes at the right side in the rear of the camp."

"I'll make sure he knows that," Jennifer said. She dug her heels into the horse's side and raced away. He waited till she was out of sight before he began the slow, laborious crawl back to the camp. He crawled closer this time, close enough to hear and to see they had half-loaded one of the two empty wagons remaining. Odin's crew kept to themselves, he noted, and the Indians did pretty much the same. One of the questions that had lingered in his mind was answered as he listened to the renegades exchange brief comments with each other. The Kiowa and the Apache tongues were related closely enough for them to understand each other. The southern Arapaho and the Cheyenne used enough Crow, the language spoken most by white traders, so they could communicate. The Wichita had to use sign language and whatever Crow they knew.

Broken Knife had himself a motley crew but they managed to work together, bound by the knowledge that they were all outcasts and their leader's talk of taking over his tribe one day. As Broken Knife slid into his thoughts, the renegade leader moved into his sight, his near-naked, powerfully built figure moving with easy grace, his cruel slash of a mouth barking an order at his men. They quickly began to start a cooking fire as dusk turned to dark. Fargo's glance went to the children, lingering on the oldest girls. They were frightened, with faces pale and staring eyes, but nothing more seemed to have been done to them. That was understandable. The better condition they were in, the better price they'd fetch.

Fargo swore under his breath. The grisly pact still had pieces that needed filling in. Was selling off the children payment enough for the renegades? Or was there something more? The Indian had no need for currency. Payment had to be something he could use for himself or for trade. But this group couldn't even trade with other tribes, Fargo pondered. Payment had to be something they could trade with the white man or enjoy for themselves. He set aside further wondering and watched as the braves brought out skinned rabbit to roast over the small fire while Odin's men settled down with food from their packs.

Broken Knife seemed in good spirits, Fargo noted. The renegade chief joked with his men and sat around the fire as the meat roasted. The braves began a steady chatter among themselves, languages intermixed. They were all in good spirits, plainly pleased at the apparent conclusion of another transaction. *Enjoy yourselves. It'll be your last time,* Fargo thought. His concentration was full on the scene in front of him, and the voices of the Indian braves were loud. He didn't pick up a sound until it was too late and he cursed in bitter anger as the voice cut into his thoughts.

"Don't move, you bastard," it said and Fargo stiffened. He heard the steps and heard the camp fall silent. Broken Knife had leaped to his feet and was staring toward him. A foot came down heavily on his back. Fargo winced as he felt the Colt yanked from his pocket and the foot leave his back. He turned and looked up to see Aran Tooney's heavy shape looming over him from behind a big Smith & Wesson

161

seven-shot, single-action. "Get up," Tooney said and Fargo pushed to his feet as Broken Knife and the others crashed through the brush to halt in surprise. "Walk," Tooney said and stepped behind Fargo, the revolver aimed at his back.

Fargo cursed his own carelessless as he walked into the camp with Broken Knife and the other Indians dancing around him. He saw Odin's men step forward. Or were they Odin's men, he questioned now. Tooney faced him with a snarling smirk. "When you said you had a lead I figured you'd find this place. That's why they call you the Trailsman," the man said. "I waited a spell this morning and then came up here. Nobody knows I'm here. Jennifer went to town." Fargo said nothing but allowed himself a moment of bitter anticipation. "Get another stake and tie him to it," Tooney ordered.

"Why not just put holes in him now?" one of the other men asked.

Tooney's eyes were narrowed. "I want to be sure he didn't get to anybody. This way we got us one more hostage. Nothing happens, we get rid of him come morning." Three of the men dragged Fargo back to the rear edge of the encampment as two others pounded a piece of branch into the ground to serve as a stake. Fargo was pulled down and bound in a sitting position to the stake with a length of lariat that pinned his arms to his sides. He stared up at Tooney as the man looked down at him with obvious relish.

"Where's Joe Odin fit in with this?" Fargo asked.

"He doesn't. He doesn't even store his wagons at my place. I rent them from him," Tooney said. Fargo decided to press questions — the man was in a victorious, confident mood.

"What the hell do you do with household stuff?" he asked.

Tooney laughed in his heavy, gravelly voice. "Sell it for real good money," he answered.

"Where?" Fargo questioned skeptically.

"Way down south of Sonora. The Mexicans come across the border with nothing but their sombreros and their shawls. Most of them have never seen real chairs and tables, to say nothing of sewing machines and good hurricane lamps. A whole village will pool their pesos to buy the stuff. Of course, I see to it that they exchange their pesos for silver or gold before I sell," Tooney said.

"And the children?" Fargo asked.

"I've special buyers waiting for them across the border," Aran Tooney smirked.

"You're a real sonofabitch, aren't you?"

Fargo commented and received a kick in his ribs.

"But I'm going to be a live one tomorrow while you'll be eating dirt, Mister Trailsman," Tooney snarled.

"How are you going to explain that to Jennifer?" Fargo asked. "She knows I've been out looking for the children."

"You'll just disappear. She'll have to accept the fact that you made a mistake and paid for it," Tooney said.

Fargo's eyes went back to where Broken Knife had sat down at the fire again with his other renegades. "How do you keep them working for you?" he asked.

"Whiskey, cousin, good whiskey," Aran Tooney said. "They're hooked on it. They'll do whatever I want so long as I keep them supplied in whiskey. Of course, Broken Knife has his own plans to be a big chief some day. He expects I'll help him in that when the time comes."

"Meanwhile, you're keeping them happy with whiskey while they massacre wagon trains for you," Fargo said.

"That keeps them happy, too." Aran Tooney laughed and Fargo felt the hatred inside himself curl into a tight knot. "Come morning, I leave with the wagons and my crew and another one of my men delivers the whiskey a few hours later. That'll be enough to keep them on a binge till I get back."

"When you start it all over again," Fargo bit out.

"Bull's-eye," Tooney crowed and Fargo reminded himself to keep a special bullet for the man. Broken Knife was a savage and bloodthirsty man but in reality he was only a tool. Aran Tooney pulled the bloodstained strings. One more question hung in Fargo's mind.

"You've got this neat little scheme going. Why'd you ask Jennifer to come out and invest with you?" he pushed at the man.

"Oh, I know this'll all come to an end one of these days. With Jennifer's money I can go back to ranching if I've a mind to. As a respectable citizen, too," Tooney said and laughed again, plainly pleased with himself.

"You figure Jennifer will never know anything about this," Fargo said.

"That's right, 'less she finds out by accident," Tooney said.

"In which case you'll take care of her, too," Fargo said and Tooney shrugged away the remark.

"You won't have to be worrying about that, Fargo. You rode your last trail this time," the man said, starting to turn away.

"How'd you hook up with that renegade?" Fargo asked.

"My woman, she's a cousin," Tooney said and sat down beside Broken Knife at the fire. He swore softly. Aran Tooney was wrong about who'd ridden the last trail, he muttered silently. Or who held the last card. Smugness was something he seldom allowed himself, but he'd make an exception this time.

7

Fargo drew a deep breath to help him relax as he watched Aran Tooney spend time with Broken Knife and with his own crew. The man strolled over at one point to stare at the children with a kind of obscene satisfaction and Fargo felt the anger boil up inside himself again. Tooney had the Colt wedged inside his belt. The children stared back at Tooney. They were silent, Fargo observed, showing no emotion and his heart went out to them. Fear had dulled emotion, exhaustion drained the body of strength and the soul despaired. He had seen them look at him and wanted to convey some gesture or word of hope. But he hadn't dared and he looked away as he saw Broken Knife coming toward him.

The Indian halted to look down at him, the cruel slash of a mouth made more so by a sneer. "You are the one," he said. "You took her that morning." Fargo smiled and received a kick in the ribs. He refused to wince. "I will kill you myself," the Indian snarled. "Tooney says you will be mine."

"He's always been the generous sort," Fargo said. The Indian frowned uncomprehendingly for a moment, then kicked him in the ribs again. Once more, Fargo refused to wince but it was getting harder to do each time. Broken Knife walked away, his powerful body rippling and returned to where the fire had begun to burn low. Fargo watched him take a blanket and begin to settle down for the night. The others followed his example. Fargo's glance went to the wagons where Tooney and his crew were also bedding down, some leaning against the wagon wheels, others stretching out beneath the big rigs. He watched as he waited and before an hour passed the camp had become a sleeping place, the silence broken only by assorted snores and snorts.

He glanced over at where the children were tied to the stakes. They, too, slept, their small bodies sagging against their bonds. Sleep was a refuge for them, a dark, private place where hope could be harbored. He swore silently and let his eyes move to the darkness of the trees across the encampment. He strained his ears, trying to pick up the sound of charging horses. But there was only silence. It was early yet, he realized and let his eyes close as he put his head back.

He dozed for a spell, woke up with a sharp

start and strained his ears again. But he heard no sounds from inside the blackness of the trees. He glanced up to see that the moon had begun its trackless path across the blue-velvet sky. It was time for Jennifer to arrive with the major and his troops, Fargo frowned. But he put away his impatience. One wrong turn in the night could cost them a half hour to correct, he realized and he forced himself to close his eyes again. He managed to doze some more and this time, when he snapped awake, his first glance was skyward. The frown spread across his forehead as he saw how far the moon had traveled. He brought his eyes down to the trees, inclining his head as he strained his ears. Only the night sounds came to him — a skulk of foxes chattering in the distance, the click of night beetles, the soft scurrying of claws against dirt and rock — long-tailed weasel or raccoon, he guessed.

Jennifer should have arrived with Major London and his platoon by now. Perhaps she had gotten herself lost. Perhaps she had to backtrack and start over to find the trail marks he'd outlined. He turned the answers in his mind and decided they were reasonable. She could need another hour, perhaps two, he decided. It would mean there had been mistakes, too many of them, but mistakes were all too possible. He leaned his head back again, closed his eyes and returned to waiting. But he felt the queasiness inside his stomach, a sign that reason and alarm clashed inside him. He swore silently and kept his eyes closed with an effort.

Another hour had passed when he pulled his eyes open again and saw the moon starting to slide toward the distant end of the black sky. He cursed silently. Something had gone wrong. They should have been here by now, even allowing for mistakes. Maybe she had never reached the major, Fargo pondered. If so, the morning would bring only victory for Aran Tooney and his devil's pact. Victory for Aran Tooney, satisfaction for Broken Knife, slavery for the children and death for himself, Fargo muttered. Something had gone wrong. Had her horse fallen as she raced the animal too fast? Had she run afoul of a hunting party of braves? Had he been wrong to send her in the first place?

Maybe he should have gone himself and never brought her along. Something had gone wrong and maybe it was as much his fault as anyone's. He cursed silently. Blaming himself wouldn't help anything. Nothing would, now. He tightened his wrists and strained forearm muscles, trying to twist his upper body without making noise. But he stopped, the rope cutting into his arms. He'd been tied with absolute efficiency. He sat quietly and let the bitterness flood over him and he suddenly knew the meaning of despair. He struggled to loosen the ropes again and once more stopped when he felt the trickle of blood on his skin.

He had just cursed silently again when he caught the sound directly behind him, a soft, rustling sound he would not have heard if he hadn't been awake. He held his breath and the sound came again, the rustle of leaves and he tried futilely to turn his head to see behind him. The sound came again, changed slightly in tone, footsteps sliding through grass. Good God, the major couldn't have quietly sneaked a platoon this close. That was simply impossible. He listened to the sliding sound and suddenly a hand clamped over his mouth.

He turned his head sideways to see Jennifer, her dark green shirt wet with perspiration and clinging to the curve of her breasts. She withdrew her hand from his mouth as she cast a quick, fearful glance around the campsite. He held back the questions that fought to leap from his lips as Jennifer started to untie the knots in the ropes that bound him. He felt her struggle, fingers fumbling as she fought with the knots that had been tightened by his struggles. She paused when she saw him shake his head. He drew his right leg up, moved it back and forth and nodded downward with his head, not daring to utter even a single word.

She frowned at him for a moment and he moved his leg again, a sideways motion and she leaned over, ran her hand across his knee and down to the calf. She halted when her fingers touched the object inside his Levis, her eyes widening. Then she was pulling his Levis up, closing her hand around the holster that encircled his calf. She pulled the slender throwing knife from the holster and immediately attacked the ropes with its double-edged blade. He felt the bonds shred in seconds and the lariat fall from his sides.

He rose slowly and carefully and Jennifer handed the thin blade back to him. He silently returned it to the calf holster as his glance swept the camp once more. It was still a sleeping place. He moved in a crouch, covering the dozen feet to the line of trees at the rear of the site, Jennifer behind him. He made his way slowly and soundlessly through the forest and halted only when he'd traveled some fifty yards from the encampment. He turned to Jennifer. Then his eyes bored into her. "What the hell happened?" he hissed. "Where's London and his damn platoon? On his way? Back somewhere waiting for a signal?"

She shook her head. "No. He's not here

and he's not coming. There are no troops. I came back alone," she said.

He stared at her and wanted to believe he had heard wrong. Her grave face told him he hadn't. "Why, goddammit," he rasped.

"There were less than a dozen men in the camp. The major had been ordered south to go after a Kiowa war party that's on a rampage. They're not expected back for another three days and the few men in the camp are under orders to stay there," Jennifer told him. "Not that they'd do us much good, anyway. So I came back, saw the Ovaro and looked for you. When I couldn't find you I crept closer and saw you tied up."

"No troops. No saving anybody," Fargo said and his eyes moved up through the tangled canopy of leaves to see the moon just disappearing over the distant hills. The pink light of the new day was not far away and he brought his eyes back to Jennifer. "I've got some news for you, too, honey," he grunted. "Joe Odin's wagons are in that camp but he isn't with them. It's your Uncle Aran's show."

He watched Jennifer's mouth fall open and her eyes grow round with astonishment. "Aran," she breathed and Fargo quickly told her everything Tooney had confessed to him.

She was silent for a long moment after he

finished. "Of course," she said, finally. "That explains it."

"The inner feelings," Fargo said.

"Yes. No rhyme or reason to them, no shape or form, but they were there. Somehow, some way, it all lay inside me. I told you I can't explain it. I've no name for it except scary."

"You've no name for it and I've no way out of this." Fargo grimaced.

Jennifer peered through the trees in the direction of the camp. "They just go off to sell their loot and the children into God knows what while we do nothing?" she asked bitterly.

"You've any ideas on how to do something?" he queried, not hiding the harshness of his own voice.

"Try to get the children out now," Jennifer said and his glance at her was reproachful.

"When they find me gone they'll figure I somehow managed to get loose. They'll figure I'm far away by now and they won't even come looking. We try to sneak back and untie the children, we'd be caught before we get the first rope cut."

"Then we follow them come morning and wait for a better chance," Jennifer said.

"The odds won't change. You and I against eleven of them. Those are no odds for a shootout and on the road, I'll wager Tooney posts sentries come night," Fargo said.

"You can get by sentries," Jennifer returned.

He heard the despair in her voice and closed one hand around her arm and kept his voice gentle. "Yes, I have and I can," he said. "But there's a lot more here. If it were rescuing one child, even two, maybe we could pull it off. But not eight. They're not woodsmen. They won't be quiet enough."

She glanced at him with her lips tight. "Then we go back to the field post and wait for the major to get back with the platoon. I'm sure you can pick up the trail again," she said.

"What if he doesn't get back in three days? There's no guarantee of that. Or what if he comes back with his platoon all shot up? It could be a week before we can pick up their trail again and that could be too late," Fargo said.

"I'm not going to just sit here and do nothing," Jennifer said.

"We can't shoot it out on the trail with them. We can't sneak eight kids out quietly enough not to be discovered. We'd need some kind of diversion to make them take their minds off us," Fargo thought aloud. "That'll be our only chance."

"Then we've got to follow them until we find that diversion," she said.

"Damn, girl, it won't be like finding a willow tree," he said. He fell silent, lips drawn back. He didn't like the idea of following the wagons. Every hour they trailed increased their risk of being accidentally discovered. And Tooney would hold another advantage. He'd be into land that was much more open by the end of the day. The risk of their being spotted was that much greater. But he had nothing better to offer and he cursed silently as the dawn light began to roll away the night. He dropped to one knee again and pulled Jennifer down beside him. The camp became distantly visible as the morning light brightened. He could see it just clearly enough through the trees to make out the bulk of the wagons and figures that seemed tiny forms. The children were being loaded into the high-paneled, closed grocery wagon and, soon after, the line of wagons began to roll.

They moved south through the trees and were soon out of sight in the forest. Fargo's eyes moved back to the camp. Broken Knife and his renegade band were settling down to wait for the whiskey wagon. He pushed to his feet, beckoned to Jennifer and moved in a crouch back to where he had left the Ovaro. When he reached the horse he saw Jennifer's mount nearby and he pulled himself into the saddle with a frown dug deep into his brow.

Jennifer cast him a glance that carried both determination and accusation in it.

"Unless you've a better idea, I'm going to follow them. I don't care what," she said stiffly.

"You go following them from here and you'll run into some of Broken Knife's men hunting breakfast," he said and she glowered back. "They'll stay heading south. We'll make a wide circle and pick them up a few miles down," he muttered. She nodded and he saw the satisfaction slide across her face. "We'll start. That doesn't mean we keep on," he said, and she gave no answer as she swung alongside him.

He rode slowly, making a long circle. The frown stayed dug into his forehead as his thoughts churned to find some way that might give them a chance to rescue the children and stay alive. But he found his mind not unlike a wagon wheel mired in the mud, spinning but going nowhere. They had ridden for almost a half hour when they came to a small stream and Jennifer halted, slid from the saddle and dropped down beside the cold, clear water. "I've got to rest some," she said and he saw the strain in her face. "Even if it's only for a half hour."

"God, yes," Fargo said, suddenly realizing how much hard riding she had been doing and he slid down to the ground beside her. "I'm sorry. I wasn't thinking too straight. Take a couple of hours. We'll pick up their trail later," he said.

Jennifer stretched out on her back alongside the stream, her eyes half-closed. "Fill my canteen, please. It's been empty for hours," she said.

"Sure thing," Fargo nodded as he took her canteen from her saddlebag and went down to the stream with it. She had a lot of strength inside her, he realized with admiration, more than enough to match her loveliness. "I wish I could fill it with whiskey for you," he said. "You could use some extra energy."

"I know where there's a wagonload of it," Jennifer said wryly.

"Yes, so do I," Fargo agreed. "Probably just starting to roll on its way now." He finished filling the canteen and replaced the lid. "But water will have to do," he grunted and suddenly he halted, the canteen held in midair in one hand. A new furrow had suddenly dug into his forehead and there were little explosions going off inside his head. "Damn," he said, jumping to his feet. "Goddamn." He ran to Jennifer's horse, jammed the canteen into the saddlebag and was at the Ovaro in two long strides. Jennifer lifted her head to frown at him.

"What is it?" she asked.

"You rest for two hours. You need it. Then I want you to meet me someplace," he said.

"Where?"

"You remember that pond we stopped at a couple of times? There's an open road that passes alongside it, some twenty miles or so north of the ranch? Think you can find it from here?" he asked.

"Yes, I'm sure of it," she answered.

"Meet me there when you wake up," he said as he swung onto the pinto.

"Why? What's happening?" she asked, pushing up on one elbow.

"I need a drink," Fargo threw back as he wheeled the horse around.

"Dammit, Fargo," Jennifer snapped.

"Haven't time to explain now. See you later this morning," he said and sent the Ovaro into a fast gallop.

8

He allowed himself to slow to a canter after a mile as he crossed the low hills into more open land. He could make time without driving the horse so hard. Time. He turned the word over in his mind. That was all-important now. The spectre of time rose up inside him again. Loose guesses were all he had to go on. How much time for him to reach the pond. How much time to do what had to be done there. How much time till Jennifer arrived and then how much time to finish and go on.

All questions. All guesswork. But he went over each in his mind again as he rode. Time the first part of his plan. Human reactions the second part. He was guessing about that, too, but he had more confidence in that guess. That, he thought wryly, was almost a fore-gone conclusion. He swerved the pinto onto a narrow road, stayed on it until it ended in a stand of hackberry. The thick woodland slowed him and the sun was high in the sky when he emerged on the other side. He spurred the pinto on down a steep slope that most horses could never handle but saved him a half-dozen miles. Finally he glimpsed the shimmer of blue caught in the bright sunlight, another mile or so away.

The land grew flatter, tree cover less thick. It was the way a wagon loaded with whiskey would come, the only way to avoid tiring the horses before they had to climb the steep hills of the high land. The pond took shape as he neared it, a cluster of buckthorns along the opposite side of the road that bordered one side of the water. He made for the low trees, rode to a halt behind them and slid to the ground. He took a moment to step out and examine the dirt near the edge of the water. Satisfied there were no fresh wagon wheel tracks, he stepped back into the buckthorn. He'd arrived in time, his first calculation correct.

He settled down on one knee and waited perhaps another half hour when he heard the low rumble of wagon wheels coming toward him, the creak of a wagon body loaded to its limit. He rose and the big stake-sided dray came into view around a slow curve. A lone driver held the reins of four heavy horses with some Percheron blood in each. The man wore a wide-brimmed black hat to shield his face from the sun and Fargo glimpsed the sixgun at his hip. A dark brown shirt and dusty gray Levis covered the rest of him. Fargo stayed in the trees as the wagon drew opposite him before he stepped out.

"Pull up and stay away from your gun," Fargo called out as he stepped from the buckthorn holding the Sharps. The man's head swiveled toward him and Fargo saw surprise flooding a wide face with a harsh jaw and tight mouth. The man pulled back on the reins and the horses came to a halt. "Get off," Fargo said. "This side where I can see you. "

The man obeyed, pulling himself across the driver's seat and sliding to the ground. "You figure on hijacking this wagonload of whiskey, mister?" he asked.

"Something like that," Fargo said.

The man sneered. "It'll be your last hijacking," he said. "You can't make time with a wagonload of whiskey kegs and you won't get very far."

Fargo smiled. He knew exactly what the man would do if he were sent packing and he noted the saddled horse tied onto the rear of the dray. "I expect I won't, not after you tell those renegades where I hijacked you," Fargo said and saw the man's eyes widen in astonishment.

"Goddamn, who the hell are you, mister?" the man asked.

"A man of salvation," Fargo said. "Though not yours."

"You going to kill me here?" the driver frowned.

"Not unless you make me," Fargo said. "Drop your gunbelt." The man's frown stayed on his face as he obeyed. "Now take off your hat, then your shirt and trousers," Fargo said.

"What the hell is this?" the driver muttered.

"Hurry up. Time's a-wastin'," Fargo said and emphasized his words by letting the hammer click on the Sharps in his hands. The man obeyed again, pulling his shirt and trousers off to stand in his longjohns. Fargo motioned with the Sharps and the man stepped to the buckthorns. "Against that one," Fargo said, gesturing to a tree a dozen feet back of the others. The man stepped to the tree and Fargo came up alongside him. His motion with the stock of the rifle was just hard enough to send the man slumping unconscious to the ground. Fargo propped the driver up against the tree trunk where he tied the man securely.

The driver moaned and blinked just as Fargo finished the last knot. He left the man to continue coming around on his own and walked to where the big dray stood not more than a half-dozen feet from the pond, the horses standing quietly, glad for the rest. He glanced across at the driver and saw the man had fully come around and could see him from where he was bound to the tree. Fargo smiled as he undid the rope from the casks at the rear of the wagon, stepped nimbly aside as three quickly rolled off and landed in the soft soil. He stepped to the toolbox at the side of the dray, found it almost empty but came up with a chisel that he'd make do.

He stepped to the first cask on the ground, aware of the driver watching him and, using the chisel, pried the top of the cask open, working carefully so that when he finished, the top could be pressed back in place. He did the same with the other two casks on the ground and then began to pour the whiskey from each onto the soft soil. "What in goddamn are you doing?" he heard the driver roar. "Who the hell are you?"

"I told you, a man of salvation," Fargo said as he continued pouring the whiskey into the ground. "A crusader, sir. Don't you know the evils of whiskey? It's the devil's brew, an abomination on the earth."

"You some goddamn crazy preacher?" the driver shouted back. "Jesus, you can't waste all that good whiskey."

"I doubt that it's good whiskey," Fargo said as he rolled more casks from the wagon — a fact which made it less painful to spill out the casks, he admitted. Again, he carefully worked the lids off before he poured the whiskey onto the ground. He had to work with care and he realized that task was going to take far longer than he'd estimated. The sun crossed into the afternoon sky and he had three quarters of the casks emptied when Jennifer rode up, hazel eyes wide as she surveyed the scene. "You want to tell me what this is all about?" she asked as she slid to the ground.

"You start filling all those casks with water," Fargo said. "We'll talk while we work." She shrugged, bent down and began to dip the first cask into the pond and finally pulled it out when it was full. "Press the top back on tight," he said and continued emptying as she filled. "Aran Tooney said that this whiskey was going south to be used as medicine for doctors. A damn lie, like everything else he said. But he was right about one thing. It is going to be used to do good. It's going to give us a chance to save eight children."

"How?" Jennifer frowned as she put the lid back tightly on another of the casks.

"It's going to help create that diversion I said we needed," Fargo told her. "The best kind of diversion, the kind that'll be poetic justice as well."

She frowned back as she filled more casks

with water. "I don't know that I'm following you," she said.

"You will. Concentrate on getting those casks filled," he said as he emptied the last of the whiskey onto the ground. He instantly began to help Jennifer fill the emptied casks with the water and cursed as he saw how far the sun had traveled across the sky. He redoubled his efforts, ignoring the pain that came to his arms and back. Finally the big dray was piled high again with the whiskey casks. He tied the tail casks in place as Jennifer rested beside the pond for a moment.

"The place smells like a saloon," she commented.

"It'll drift away in a few hours," he said. "Now we're going to deliver a wagonload of whiskey for your Uncle Aran. Or, more accurately, you are."

Jennifer's brows lifted as she stood up. He pointed to the driver's clothes. "Put those duds on over your own," he said. "Pin your hair up and put his hat on."

Jennifer's eyes grew narrow as she picked up the man's trousers and started to draw them on. "I think it's all coming together now," she said. "But what if they see it's not him?"

"I'm betting they won't give you a second look," Fargo said. "I'm sure they never pay any attention to him when he brings the wagon. They're too busy pulling the casks off. He just leaves the wagon, gets on that horse tied behind and rides away. They've probably got the first cask open before he's down the hillside."

She nodded as she finished pinning her hair up with a hairclip. She donned the man's wide-brimmed black hat and her face all but disappeared underneath it. He lifted the brim and looked beneath it. "What do you see?" she asked.

"The face of a young boy," Fargo said. "That's what Broken Knife will see if he should give you a look. If I were under that hat he'd recognize me and the whole thing would blow up." Jennifer climbed onto the seat of the big dray and took the reins in hand while Fargo paused to look at the driver bound to the tree.

"You just going to leave me like this?" the man protested.

"Somebody will come along in a day or two. Maybe," Fargo said. "You can tell them a good citizen stopped you from smuggling whiskey to the Indians. That's twenty years at hard labor so you ought to be grateful to me."

Fargo gathered Jennifer's mount and rode alongside the wagon as she drove off. "You expect Broken Knife is going to go after Aran when he finds the whiskey casks hold only water," she said.

"Damn right," Fargo said. "He's going to think your Uncle Aran cheated him on purpose and he's going to come looking for blood. Aran will know something went wrong the minute he sees the renegades come charging. He'll stop to put up a fight for his life."

"And we use that time to try and rescue the children," Jennifer said.

"That's the idea. It can go wrong but it's our one chance. There will be a pitched battle going on between the renegades and Tooney's men. Broken Knife won't give a damn about the kids. Not till after he's finished with Tooney and Tooney's crew will be too busy trying to stay alive to bother about the kids. It'll be the best chance we'll have, maybe the only one," Fargo said and cast a sidelong glance at her. "The best chance to lose our scalps, too," he added. Nothing changed in the determination in her face, he noted and he led the way up a low hill with a passage wide enough for the wagon.

The sun had moved farther down the sky when they finally rolled slowly through the heavy forest terrain that bordered the renegade camp. Fargo's eyes swept the foliage ahead of them, the camp not more than another half-mile distant. "I'll be leaving the

188

horses here," he said. "When you get into the camp you leave the wagon and get onto the horse tied on back. Move slowly, easily, just the way the regular driver would." Jennifer nodded and his eyes swept the foliage once more. "You ride out of the camp, no hurrying, just come back this way." She nodded again and Fargo slowed the Ovaro and let Jennifer roll on. He moved from the rudimentary passageway and into the trees, risked going on another thousand yards and drew to a halt. He heard Jennifer move through the foliage with the heavy wagon and he dismounted to move another hundred yards closer on foot.

He saw the foliage moving where the wagon passed through and then he lost sight of everything and halted to let his ears become his eyes. Straining his ears, he managed to pick up the sounds of voices. The wagon had arrived in the camp and the voices rose in pitch, taking on a note of excitement. Jennifer would be moving back to the horse, now, he told himself, trying to see what was happening in his thoughts. They'd be starting to unload the dray, now, and Jennifer was swinging onto the horse, untying the reins and slowly wheeling in a circle.

The Indians were still pulling casks from the wagon, perhaps rolling them toward the center of camp. Jennifer would be out of the camp now, he pictured through half-closed eyes. She'd urge the horse on a little faster now and he heard more excited voices drifting through the trees. He pulled his eyes open and glanced upward. The sun had passed over the distant hills. The purple-gray of dusk was descending quickly. Darkness would follow even more quickly in the denseness of the forest. He rose and peered through the foliage. Where the hell was she, he swore when suddenly, he caught the movement of a branch, then another and Jennifer came into sight. He stepped out in front of her just as he heard the wild half-scream, half-shout from the camp.

The shout rose in pitch, became a roar of anger as he trotted alongside Jennifer. "They've found the water," he said. "We've some time. They'll check more of the casks." He reached the Ovaro and Jennifer transferred to her own mount. Fargo heard another roar rising in the distance — furious anger, unmistakable, even so distant. "They've sampled other casks. They know they've been taken, now," Fargo said as he led Jennifer into the deep trees and the darkness closed in on them.

"Will they go after the wagons now?" Jennifer asked.

He glanced at the near-blackness that had

descended. "I doubt it. They'll wait till daylight. They know they can catch them tomorrow," he said. "And we'll bed down right here and wait." He drew her deeper into the trees and helped swing her from the saddle. When the moon rose, it permitted a fitful pale light that let him unsaddle the horses and stretch out his bedroll. Jennifer took off the man's clothes and threw them into the brush as she came to lie down beside him.

From the distance, they could hear the faint sound of drums and voices raised in chants from time to time. "They're invoking the spirits to help them revenge being cheated," Fargo said. "Every tribe has their own chants and their own customs. This bunch is putting together their own hodgepodge. The price of being renegades."

"And tomorrow they'll take out all their anger on Uncle Aran," Jennifer said.

"That's fine with me," Fargo said harshly. "A lot of dead men, women and children will agree with that."

"Yes," Jennifer said. "I can't find any sympathy for him. I guess I'm sorry I ever came out to visit him. Except for one thing." He didn't need to ask further as her lips found his with soft, lingering sweetness.

"You came and you're doing more than you need to do," he told her. "You don't need to apologize for anything to anybody."

Her hand crept inside his shirt, rested against his chest and she offered her lips again before she drew away. "I want to so much but I can't. Not here, not with them so close," she said.

"I understand," he said.

"Afterwards," she said. "Promise me? Afterwards. It was so wonderful."

♦ "Count on it," he told her and she curled up tight against him. His hand moved inside her shirt to cup one soft breast and she uttered a contented little sigh as she let sleep come to her. He lay still, holding her and swore softly to himself. She had no idea what the chances were of pulling off what they planned. Perhaps it was best she didn't, he pondered. He knew and one could worry enough for two. Timing would be crucial once again. If they delayed too long, if one or the other got the upper hand, it would fail. They had to move when the fighting was in full swing. It meant they also had to be in position. He pushed aside further thoughts as the distant drums finally stopped. Only the night sounds remained and he closed his eyes and slept with Jennifer in his arms.

The morning sun woke him as it filtered down through the thick foliage to speckle the ground with little spots of yellow. He felt

Jennifer stir and saw her eyes come open as he rose to his feet. He brought the canteens from the horses and when they finished washing away sleep, he cocked his head to one side to listen. Sounds from the camp drifted through the trees, voices raised and lowered. Then other ones raised and he managed to recognize one. Soon after he picked up the soft thud of unshod pony hooves and the low rumbling of horses brushing through foliage, rubbing against each other.

"They're on their way," he said and began to saddle the Ovaro as Jennifer hurried to saddle her mount. He led the way when she was ready, skirted the encampment and followed the trail to the renegade band. They were moving fast and Fargo stayed well back, able to follow just by sound. The Indians rode hard and they paused only once late in the day to let their ponies drink at a stream. Fargo let them go on before he paused at the spring and watched Jennifer as she climbed from the saddle. "Can you go on?" he asked and she nodded. He rode south after the Indian band and the terrain grew harsher, with less tree cover and more open land with sandstone rock formations.

He took the high land along the back side of the rocks where he could still see the racing renegades as they cut through a pass between two tall rock pinnacles. He stayed well back even though the Indian band was intent on pursuit and little else. A series of tall rock formations rose up as the land grew dryer, small clusters of black oak lining a half-dozen passages through the rock. They were well into Texas, Fargo knew and he chose a high path that brought them almost parallel to the renegades below. He raised his arm suddenly and pointed into the distance. Jennifer peered forward and he saw her nod excitedly as the line of wagons took shape.

It wouldn't take the renegade band more than ten minutes to reach Tooney's wagons, Fargo estimated. Tooney would hear them in five and he was in terrain open enough for him to bring his wagons to the rocks and make a stand. Fargo motioned to Jennifer and put the Ovaro into a full gallop along the high passage. The renegades were unaware he passed them above as they streaked across the terrain below. Fargo's eyes searched the land forms ahead until he spotted a passage downward.

Jennifer rode beside him as he sent the pinto down. He could see the wagons clearly now. His eyes narrowed as he found the closed grocery wagon second in line and Aran Tooney riding beside it. As he watched, he saw Tooney suddenly spin in his saddle and peer back. The man had caught the sound of pounding hoofs on the hard-packed dry soil. Fargo slowed the Ovaro; he was reaching the bottom of the passage too quickly. He saw the shocked surprise on Aran Tooney's jowly face as Broken Knife and his renegades charged into sight. A dozen questions had to be exploding in Tooney's head, Fargo was certain, but he saw Tooney instantly realize that he had no time for questions.

Whatever the reasons, he was being attacked and he screamed orders at his men who scrambled frantically to draw the wagons into a half-circle against a high wall of granite to protect their backs. But Broken Knife was charging full out, his warriors splitting the air with war whoops and Fargo saw two of Tooney's men cut down by six arrows before they could leap from their wagon. The Indians made a passing sweep, pouring a hail of arrows and some bullets into the wagons. Another of Tooney's crew went down with an arrow through his collarbone. The men settled down enough to get off an answering volley and two of the Indians fell from their ponies. But the others were sweeping back again. They fired another hail of arrows and some more bullets, but Tooney's men brought down two more.

Fargo swore softly as he saw the sides of the grocery wagon splinter with the impact of six arrows and two bullets. Broken Knife was peeling away to charge again. This time he came in from the front, his warriors split into smaller groups that raced dead-on firing their arrows and then swung away. The maneuver gave the defenders less time to shoot and smaller targets to shoot at, but Tooney's men managed to bring down another two of the renegades. Broken Knife drew his men back and Fargo saw them leap from their ponies to suddenly become a horde of scurrying, crouching, darting targets.

Tooney's men were firing too fast now, missing the figures that darted and swerved, fell prone and rose up again, all the while managing to hurl arrows at their quarry. Another of Tooney's men went down with an arrow protruding from the base of his neck. Fargo motioned to Jennifer as he took the pinto along a narrow pathway that crossed behind the tall granite slab. He slowed when he reached the other end, the sounds of the battle echoing through the rocks, and he saw another of Tooney's crew fall. Broken Knife's warriors were swarming now, like so many fire ants. "This is going to turn one-sided in another two minutes," he said to Jennifer. "We've got to move now." He reined to a halt, pulled the big Sharps from its saddlecase and tossed it to her. "Ride near and take out anyone who chases after me," he called, turned and raced toward the paneled grocery wagon.

One of Tooney's men at the rear wheel of the wagon heard him coming, spun and started to bring his revolver to bear. Fargo heard the Sharps's fire from behind him and the man flew backward in an explosion of red. Fargo waved a hand in approval as he vaulted into the driver's seat of the grocery van and sent the two-horse team spurting forward. He crouched as low as he could and still control the wagon. He heard two arrows smash into the panel just behind his head. The sounds of the battle continued from behind him and he glanced back. Jennifer raced along a dozen feet behind him, the Ovaro following her but he saw another horse come out from behind one of the freight wagons, a heavyset, jowl-faced figure in the saddle.

Aran Tooney realized by now that his men were about to be slaughtered. He wanted to salvage something for himself. The children would bring him the most money, probably with buyers already waiting. He might also reason that Broken Knife would be satisfied with wiping out the others. That could be an error, Fargo knew as he swerved the wagon around a high pinnacle of rock. He glanced back, saw Aran Tooney closing fast, a revolver raised in one hand. He looked across at Jennifer where she raced almost parallel with Tooney but on the other side of the wagon. She had brought the rifle to her shoulder but she didn't fire.

"Shoot, dammit," Fargo swore into the wind and still Jennifer held back and he cursed again. She was having trouble following through. Tooney was her uncle and she was fighting with the emotions that whirled through her. Fargo shot a glance at Tooney and saw the man turn his revolver. Tooney had no trouble with family ties or the sensitivities of civilized emotions, Fargo knew. "Shoot," Fargo shouted again as he saw the revolver buck in Tooney's hand and the sound of the shot drowned out his voice.

He looked across at Jennifer and saw her go over the far side of the horse. "Goddamn," he swore as he turned the wagon toward an archway of rock. He glanced back at Jennifer again. She lay on the ground, the horse running off to the side. Fargo drove the paneled van beneath the arch of rock as Tooney swung in behind him, closing fast. The passage through the arch was just wide enough for the wagon and as he reached the far side of the rock, Fargo pulled to a halt. He leaped from the driver's seat onto a protrusion of rock and scrambled up the arch to the top. He heard Tooney curse as he had to skid to a halt inside the archway. He'd have to back out the way he'd come in and Fargo crouched at the other end of the arch, poised to jump.

The rump of Tooney's horse appeared below him and he held another split second and jumped. He landed on Tooney as the man backed out directly below him and felt the jar of the collision go through his body. He fell from the horse with Tooney, losing his grip on the man for a moment as he hit the ground. He shook cobwebs from his head, spun and saw Aran Tooney still on the ground, trying to bring his heavy, paunchy body around. But he'd held onto the revolver somehow and as Fargo started at him, he tried to bring the gun up to shoot. Fargo twisted his body as he kicked out with one leg. His foot slammed into Aran Tooney's hand and the gun flew from the man's grip just as it fired, the shot going harmlessly into the air.

Fargo, on both feet again, charged Tooney as the man managed to pull himself onto his hands and knees. Fargo aimed a slicing left hook at the jowly face, saw it open the man's eyebrow with a deep gash. But Tooney charged forward with a low tackle, both arms outstretched and Fargo felt himself go back and down as the man barreled into him at the knees. Fargo hit the ground with Aran

Tooney's head into his chest. The man used his weight to pin him in place while he brought his arms up and Fargo saw Tooney's hands reach to close around his throat.

He got one arm free, blocked Tooney's left hand and managed to bring one knee up and smash it into the man's groin. Tooney gave a gasp of pain, shifted his body a fraction but it was enough for Fargo to bring his leg up further and get the leverage he needed. He swung Tooney from atop him, scrambled away in a half-roll and glanced back to see the man half-crawling, half-diving for the sixgun. Fargo leaped to his feet, reached the gun just as Tooney's hand did. He brought his boot down on the man's hand and felt knuckles crack as Tooney screamed in pain. Fargo drew his boot away as Tooney rolled onto his back. With a curse of surprise, Fargo saw that Tooney still clutched the gun. The man's broken fingers were caught around the gun, as if welded to it. He fired as Fargo dived to the side and felt the bullet graze his back.

Fargo rolled, heard Tooney still firing, now unable to stop — his finger working in spasmodic nerve twitches. Tooney started to get to his feet, then stumbled and pitched forward. Again the gun went off. The bullet drove through Aran Tooney's paunch, through his belly and groin and, with a slow, stumbling motion, the man fell forward to lay face down on the ground, gun hand underneath him. Fargo rose as the gun fired again, a last reflex of muscle and nerves. Aran Tooney's body gave a little leap and lay still.

Fargo straightened, drew a deep breath and turned to see the bronzed, near-naked figure standing near the rock arch, bow raised, bowstring pulled back, the arrow ready to fly. "Shit," Fargo swore. A grin of evil triumph held the renegade leader's slash of a mouth and he took another step forward. Fargo glanced around and cursed again. He was completely out in the open, not a rock or tree or bush near enough to afford any kind of shelter. He brought his eyes back to the Indian. Every muscle in his body tensed and he let himself go into a half-crouch. Fargo's eyes bored into the renegade. But not at his eyes, not at the slash of a mouth. Fargo's eyes were riveted on the wrist muscles and fingers of the Indian's bowstring hand, aware that to try and run would certainly bring an arrow through his back.

He needed that split-second moment of advantage to have any chance at all. Broken Knife, confident of his position, allowed himself another step closer and Fargo remained motionless. The Indian's grin widened, certain his quarry was transfixed with fear. Fargo's eyes remained anchored to the man's wrist and fingers and suddenly he saw the ripple of the wrist muscle, fingers starting to uncurl. He flung himself sideways as the arrow left the bow, no chance for the shooter to correct its path. Fargo dived, knowing all too well that the distance was too close, the arrow hurtling without the whisper of a wind to disturb it. He hit the ground and heard his quick cry of pain as the arrow struck into the back of his left shoulder. It was a sideswipe blow — yet enough to let the sharp arrowhead cut into him.

He rolled, his shoulders throbbing with pain, turned onto his side and started to push to his feet as the near-naked figure came flying at him with a scream of fury. Fargo saw the jagged-edged skinning knife in the man's hand, the kind of blade that could tear muscle and sinew. He flung himself sideways again in another half-roll and felt the knife tear along the back of his shirt collar as Broken Knife landed. Fargo scrambled, trying to regain his feet again but managed to turn only enough to see the Indian diving at him with the ugly bladed weapon raised. On his back, Fargo had only time to draw one leg up and kick out straight with all his strength. The blow caught Broken Knife in the chest with enough power to make him grunt in pain as it deflected his dive. He landed alongside Fargo but his forward momentum was not entirely stopped and Fargo cursed in pain again as the skinning knife came down against the side of his thigh.

He felt the stain of warm wetness on his leg as he rolled away and regained his feet just as the Indian came up, moving toward him with the knife poised to slash out. Fargo circled, aware that his strength and reflexes had been sapped by the battle with Tooney and the pain in his thigh and shoulder would soon weaken him further. The renegade came at him with light, dancing steps, his eyes glittering with hatred. Fargo avoided a tentative thrust of the knife, avoided another and was able to twist away from a real slicing blow. He went backward, circled again and leaped back from another arc of the knife aimed at slashing his abdomen in two.

Out of the corner of his eye Fargo saw the archway of rock and as he circled, he moved closer to it. Intent on slicing him with the blade, certain that Fargo was slowing and one of the blows would soon land, the renegade didn't take notice that Fargo had managed to maneuver within a dozen feet of the high stone arch. He thrust again with the skinning knife, a forward jab this time and Fargo barely avoided the blow. As Broken Knife moved left, then right, feinting with his feet, Fargo cast a quick glance at the stone arch. It wouldn't offer a hiding place but it could afford enough protection to ease the relentless pressure the Indian was exerting with the constant slicing blows.

His lips tightening, Fargo decided he was close enough and he suddenly spun and ran, ignoring the pain in his thigh as he drove his legs forward. Broken Knife had been taken by surprise, losing precious seconds before he recovered and gave chase. He was fast, Fargo saw, and closing ground but the stone arch was within reaching. Fargo swerved to round the nearest side when he felt his foot smash into the protrusion of rock. He screamed out a curse as he went down. He had time only to turn and get his hands up to meet the renegade's dive. He managed to close his fingers around the man's wrist and hold the knife inches away from plunging into him. Broken Knife, on top of him, tried to bring more weight to bear but the rocky surface was smooth and he lost his footing. He began to roll and Fargo rolled with him, not daring to let go of the wrist.

Both figures rolled together, over and over down the slight slope at one side of the arch. The Indian was screaming curses and Fargo desperately clung to his grip on the man's wrist. But the pain across his shoulder was excruciating, draining strength from him. When they stopped rolling, Broken Knife pulled his other arm free and smashed a blow downward. Fargo twisted his head away just in time to avoid the blow smashing into his face. But his grip on the Indian's wrist had slackened for a split-second and Broken Knife tore his arm free.

He came down with his other arm, jamming his forearm into Fargo's throat as, with a scream of triumph, he raised the knife to plunge it down and end the battle. Fargo cursed as he realized he was pinned down, the Indian's forearm cutting off breath and strength. The shot rang out just as Broken Knife was about to plunge the skinning knife downward. The bullet missed but it came close enough to graze the Indian's thick black hair. Broken Knife ducked and half-turned in astonishment, bringing his forearm up in a reflex action. Fargo knew he had been given a large desperate moment of reprieve and he took it. His wide, swinging arc of a blow delivered as he lay on his back, landed against the side of the Indian's head. No real power was behind it, yet it was enough to send the man toppling sideways. Fargo leapt up as the renegade hit the ground. This time his blow carried real power as he drove a crackling left hook into the Indian's jaw. Broken Knife's head snapped backward as he fell back. He hit the ground and the knife fell from his fingers.

He spun, dived for it, but Fargo reached it first, closing his hand around the blade and the renegade's arm tried to come around his neck from behind. Fargo swung his arm backward without aiming, executing a short, quick arc. He felt the knife tear into flesh and heard the man's guttural gasp of pain. He brought the knife forward, felt it tear along more flesh and the renegade fell backward, his arm falling away. Fargo tore free and spun to see the renegade sinking to his knees, both hands clutching his abdomen where a torrent of red poured through the shreds of torn muscle and sinew. He fell forward and lay still. Fargo whirled to peer past the stone arch where the shot had come from. He felt the shout well up inside him as he saw the figure on the horse, dusty-blond hair made brighter in the last of the sun.

He ran forward shouting and the horse moved toward him, the rider sliding to the ground as he reached and his arms were around her, holding her tight. "If ever there was a sight for sore eyes," he said. "You went down. I thought Tooney had taken you out."

"His shot missed but I was trying to duck low. I lost my balance and fell. I hit my head and passed out," Jennifer said. "When I came to I saw my horse had stopped only a few yards away so I climbed back on. Tooney had been chasing you in this direction so I followed. When I saw the grocery van under the arch I knew I'd reached the last stop. I was afraid of what else I'd find."

Fargo pulled back, his face tight. "Were they still fighting? Could you hear when you came after me?" he asked.

"Maybe a shot or two," she said and he nodded grimly. He saw the renegade leader's pony standing nearby and strode to the horse. He led the animal by the rope bridle, down to where the Indian lay lifeless on the ground. He lifted the man and flung him sideways across the horse's back. He walked to Aran Tooney, pushed the man's thick body over with his boot and retrieved the Colt and dropped it into his holster where it belonged.

He walked up the slight incline toward the stone arch, leading the Indian pony behind him and left the horse and its lifeless rider as he opened the rear door of the van with Jennifer. The eight small figures lay on the floor of the van, some huddled into the corners. They stared back with wide eyes, small faces unsmiling and made blank with fear. "It's over," he said and silently hoped he was right. "You're safe." They made no reply, their wide-eyed faces just staring at him and he cursed under his breath as he turned to Jennifer. "It's a kind of shock," he said. "Sometimes it takes weeks to come out of it. They'll be better when we get them to the Doc at Red Sand."

"I'll drive," she said. "I'll open the front panel behind the driver's seat and leave the rear doors open so they can look out."

He nodded and walked to the Ovaro which had halted just the other side of the stone arch. After he swung into the saddle and turned the horse around, he waited while Jennifer drove the van from beneath the arch and turned alongside him. That was when he saw the riders moving toward them. Half the number they had once been. "You stay here," he said as he moved forward, took the pony with Broken Knife's body across it and slowly rode forward. He halted as the Indians came up to him, dropped the rope bridle and sent the horse moving toward them with a soft slap on its rump.

The Indians started at the lifeless form across the pony and Fargo waited, his eyes hard, one hand on the Colt. Two of the Indians, one with Wichita markings on his headband, glanced over at him. He kept his face as still as stone. They did what he expected they would as they took the pony with them and slowly turned away. He stayed, watching, waiting until they disappeared from sight before turning to Jennifer and the van.

"They're finished. They'll go off, each to his own. Some may try to return to their tribes. They're not a renegade band anymore. They're just outcasts," he said.

He rode beside Jennifer as she sent the van rolling forward. The trip back was slow and they camped for the night and he had the children sit around a small fire. They obeyed with the same wordlessness and Jennifer saw to it that they stayed by the warmth of the fire as they slept. "Now for you," she said and applied bandages made from his shirt to his thigh as he undressed. "The shoulder will need some salve," she said. He directed her to his saddlebag and when she'd finished applying the ointment the burning quickly stopped along his shoulder blade.

She was sitting quietly beside him, staring into the fire, when he heard the sound, soft at first, then louder, a murmured sobbing. It came from a little boy at the end of the circle and Jennifer ran to the child. He watched as she cradled the child in her arms. Another stifled sob broke loose, a girl this time, and she came into Jennifer's arms. Fargo listened to the sobs. No terror in them but the feel of relief and joy, the sound of the unlocking of the heart.

Finally, the small forms were silent again and asleep beside the fire. Jennifer returned to him. "They're going to be fine, all of them. It may take a little longer with some but they'll be fine. Getting them to town and a doctor will help."

"We should make it by tomorrow late," he said. He finished undressing and lay down on his bedroll naked. Jennifer moved away to lie down alone. "Why?" he frowned.

"You're not fit for anything and my self-discipline isn't that good," she said.

"I'll be fit come tomorrow night," he said.

"And I won't have a damn shred of self-discipline left by then," she said. He smiled as he closed his eyes and welcomed sleep.

Her words proved true the next night after they had taken the children back into town. "Not at Aran's place," she said. "The inn in town." He agreed and understood. But she proved her words true. The kind of proving he'd not forget for a long time. But then, those who discover a new taste always want more of it. And good deeds deserved being rewarded, he told himself as he pressed his face into her breasts. And some rewards were better than others.

The employees of Thorndike Press hope you have enjoyed this Large Print book. All our Large Print titles are designed for easy reading, and all our books are made to last. Other Thorndike Press Large Print books are available at your library, through selected bookstores, or directly from the publishers.

For more information about titles, please call:

(800) 257-5157

To share your comments, please write:

Publisher
Thorndike Press
P.O. Box 159
Thorndike, Maine 04986